Lenters

IF ALL THE SWORDS IN ENGLAND

Also by the Author

If all the Swords in England

By

BARBARA WILLARD

ILLUSTRATED BY

Robert M. Sax

BETHLEHEM BOOKS · IGNATIUS PRESS

BATHGATE, N.D.   SAN FRANCISCO

First Bethlehem Books edition, June 2000
Second printing, May 2001

ISBN: 1–883937–49–3
Library of Congress Card Number: 00–102322

Bethlehem Books • Ignatius Press
10194 Garfield Street South
Bathgate, ND 58216
www.bethlehembooks.com

Printed in the United States on acid free paper

TABLE OF CONTENTS

Introduction

THIS HISTORICAL novel, *If All The Swords In England* by Barbara Willard, justly deserves to see the light of day again and to be enjoyed by a new generation of youthful keen historians. As in her book, *Augustine Came To Kent,* Miss Willard has chosen to tell the story of an Archbishop of Canterbury, this time Saint Thomas Becket. All children who have ever studied medieval English history can recite from memory the ominous words of the King, Henry II Plantagenet, as he sought to destroy the great churchman, "Will no one rid me of this turbulent priest?" (As a child, it was probably my first introduction to the usage of the word "turbulent").

The story of Thomas Becket's quarrel with his King and its tragic and far-reaching conclusion is the very stuff of history, drama and the imagination. In recent times it has inspired both a film, *Becket,* and a great (American-born) poet, T.S. Eliot, to write his religious drama, *Murder In The Cathedral.* Here, Miss Willard expertly weaves the killing of the Archbishop in his own cathedral by four Norman knights anxious to curry favour with their master, into a narrative spanning the years 1164-1170.

The action is seen through the eyes of two boys, twins, high born but orphaned, as they seek their fortunes in the world: one in the service of the King, the other in the service of his former chancellor and now Archbishop of Canterbury (the premier bishop in England), Thomas Becket. One brother, Simon, has a withered left hand, which has its own significance in the story. The other brother, Edmund, desperately tries, but fails, to avert the consequences of the King's furious appeal. The story takes place both in England and France, reminding one that in those days English kings ruled more of France than the French kings themselves. The descriptions of dress, custom, court and monastic life are realistic and vivid. Young readers today will discover that the status of "childhood" as a privileged time of growth and development did not exist in twelfth century Europe. Children then often had to fend for themselves, make decisions and be mature in ways that their modern counterparts could hardly imagine. But of course children love to imagine just this: how they, pretending to be the heroes of such stories, would cope in those strange, far-off (and turbulent) days.

In Christian families, other questions will arise from reading this story. What comes first, loyalty to a human ruler, or loyalty to God? What part does conscience play in making important decisions? What qualities of courage and perseverance are needed when you have to stand, seemingly alone, against a hostile and powerful enemy? What is more important, preserving a friendship or standing up for the truth?

All the ingredients are there, in this absorbing tale: two men, both of great ability and powers of leadership, who once were the best of friends; the slow death of their friendship in a quarrel over their mutual claim to a particular juridical authority; the colourful backdrop of medieval Europe, which was still—unlike today, alas—an organic, living Christian world. Miss Willard shows a society in which God is very present in every aspect of life: in the observance of feast days and fasts, in the universal horror of sacrilege—as in the slaughter of a priest at his own altar; in the need to make amends when one has done wrong. King Henry's very public humiliation and penitence is itself a lesson in how human authority should mean "service" but often becomes "tyranny."

The clash between a King and his subject in this story is a fateful intimation of a later, even more famous clash, that between Henry VIII and another Thomas, Thomas More—later, like Becket, a saint. Becket's words in this story, "I will submit in all things—saving God's honour," are hardly different from the cheerful words of Thomas More on the scaffold: "I die the King's good servant—but God's first." Thomas Becket was murdered on 29 December 1170 in Canterbury Cathedral. Until the Reformation, which tragically divided Christendom, his shrine at Canterbury was one of the principal places of pilgrimage in Europe (other popular sites were Rome, Santiago de Compostela, Spain, and Walsingham, England). Thousands of people (immortalised in Chaucer's wonderful *Canterbury Tales*) came to Canterbury to pray. There they remembered the life of one man, who chose martyrdom rather than submit to what he regarded as the unlawful demands of a secular sovereignty. To-day too, young Christian readers in the western world can learn a valuable lesson from the historical events described in these pages: that they, in their own lives, must sometimes stand up and be counted in the service of Christ, Who is Lord of all history.

FRANCIS PHILLIPS
Aylesbury, England
April, 2000

"If all the swords in England were pointed against my head, your threats could not move me."

Thomas Becket to his murderers

England & France
A.D. 1170

ENGLAND
London
Sandwich
Canterbury
Dover
Calais
Boulogne

ENGLISH CHANNEL

ENGLISH POSSESSIONS IN FRANCE

Rouen
Seine
Paris
Marne
Montmirail
Seine
Yonne
Sens
Pontigny
Orleans
Angers
Loire
Nantes

ATLANTIC OCEAN

I

A Place in the King's Household, 1164

"THE TALLER LAD will do very well," said the steward, "but I cannot offer the other a place."

This was entirely unexpected. For a second Oliver seemed to be completely at a loss. He had brought

1

the two boys all the way from Wales to London to take service with the King. It was what their dead father would have wished, and Oliver, who had been his personal servant, had never doubted that both boys would be taken.

"They are twin-born," he said at last. "They have one mind. *The other,* as you call him, gives his brother no more than half an inch."

"All of three, if you ask," replied the steward, good-humoredly. "Twins, eh? Well, if they'd been as like in body as you say they are in mind I would have taken a chance. The King enjoys a joke. There was a time when the Queen had twin sisters among her ladies, but—well, to be blunt—a lad with one useless hand is not likely to stand much chance as a page."

At this, Edmund Audemer, the slightly taller, robuster boy, put his arm across his brother's shoulders and said sharply, "Simon is twice as nimble as I am. There was none better serving at table in my grandfather's hall. And he is clever—twice as clever as I am."

"Now do not persuade me that you lack wit," said the King's steward, "or I shall not take you, either."

Simon, who all this time had been standing beside Edmund in the silence of utter misery, now forced himself to speak up.

"My brother is only pleading for me, Master Steward. Truly I am nimble, also I am able to write and to calculate. No one will believe I can also pour wine at table and never spill a drop. But Edmund is strong and I am not. And no doubt the King needs strong men about him."

The steward looked at Simon and smiled. "May Our Lady hear me, I would take you if I could. But this is a rough world, for all it is a royal one. I am bound to say No to you. But to your brother I say Yes, if he chooses."

"I do not—" began Edmund hotly.

"He chooses," Simon said, firm and steady.

"Indeed it is best that he should," said Oliver, with a sigh. "God knows I would not force you two apart. But it is a place beside the King himself, Edmund—as your father always intended—as your mother always prayed. Riches you may have none, but you have your Norman blood to make you a place in the world."

"They are Sir Richard Audemer's sons, you say?" The King's steward looked approving. "I saw him once when we rode in Anjou. He was a knight of high distinction."

"But a poor man, alas," said Oliver. "For no other reason than dire necessity would I leave these lads and find service elsewhere. I have cared for them as though they were my own for this past year. Their father and mother died cruelly, and now their grandfather, their good mother's father who gave us shelter, is dead, too. The family estates have fallen into disrepair and so we must all seek our fortunes as best we may."

For the first time since they had entered the great

fortress-palace of the Tower of London, the two boys looked at one another. Although they were not in fact identical, they had, as Oliver claimed, one mind. So Edmund knew all the fear and loneliness that Simon experienced at the thought of parting; while Simon knew Edmund's angry wish to throw away this opportunity. And both knew that their father would have expected them to submit.

It was just a year since tragedy had broken the family. They had been riding into Wales to celebrate Christmas at the border castle of their mother's father. The small, confident cavalcade was making its way in bright, frosty weather—the parents, the ten-year-old twins, the little sister, the servants, the six or so men-at-arms. Nothing more impressive than a robber band had swept down upon them, and afterward somehow this had seemed to add disgrace to disaster. Both parents died, and with them the little sister the boys had so dearly prized.

Edmund had been riding with Oliver. In the confusion and terror they were swept away from Simon, who saw his father struck down. It was Simon who snatched at his father's hand as he died, who held it as the stir and terror of the skirmish swept over and on. The winter dark came down and still Simon lay with his hand clasping and clasped by the chill dead hand of his father. At last Oliver, limping from a sword thrust, came with Edmund and the surviving servants, half of them wounded and bleeding, searching and calling. He prised away the dead fingers and lifted up Simon, who could only sob and cry and lie across the man's shoulders with his eyes closed. . . . Though he had received no wound, Simon's left hand had been useless since that day. . . .

He looked away from Edmund now and glanced instead at this hand of his that must be the cause of their separation. But since it had been the last hand to clasp his father's he felt no bitterness, only sorrow.

"Oliver is sure to find me a place in London, Edmund," he said as hopefully as he could. "There will be all the saints' days and the festivals—then we shall meet and keep the holiday together."

"Certainly the sport in London these days should please any lad," agreed the steward. "Thank God, we are well over the troubles of King Stephen's reign. Our sovereign lord King Henry keeps the realm in peace." He clapped Edmund on the shoulder in a friendly way. "Make your farewells, then, boy—they are all the harder for keeping. Look for me in the wardrobe court in ten minutes. We must get you fitted with a livery." He nodded to Oliver. "You have done the best for him, be sure of that. He'll do well. And he'll have a place worthy of his birth." He paused as he got to the door. "The smaller lad can write, you say? It is a pity the Archbishop of Canterbury has gone from England into France. He loves a scribe and would have taken him in for sure. When great men quarrel we all must suffer, one way or the other."

The mention of the Archbishop stirred Simon deeply. He knew of him from Oliver, whose sister had married for her second husband a distant relative of the Archbishop's. He knew that he had been born Thomas Becket, that he had been Chancellor of England and the King's closest friend. He knew that when, at the King's insistence and persuasion, Thomas Becket had been ordained and consecrated Archbishop of Canterbury, there had occurred the clash of wills, the quarrel that had led to exile. But it was his grandfather's chaplain who had said to Simon: *There is a greater man in England than the King, and his name is Thomas Becket. . . .* Suddenly Simon felt certain that it was better for him to seek out the Archbishop, wherever he might be, than to wear the King's livery, as Edmund was to do.

It was as though, out of the blue, a purpose was given to the parting with his brother, and a promise of consolation.

They came out under the great archway that was so thick it was more nearly a tunnel. Their footsteps echoed on the damp stone flags. A mist sneaked in off the river in winter, and though the short day was bright, the dampness had had no time to evaporate.

"If I had known the King and the court were at Marlborough I would have taken you there," said Oliver to Simon. "A different officer might have taken you both."

Simon said nothing. In the courtyard the servant, Hodge, waited with the horses. Edmund's gray had been led away. But there was Oliver's tall chestnut, and Simon's gentle bay mare; she knew all his tricks with the reins, which he wound round his left arm, above the elbow, relying on his right hand to do all the work. Hodge rode a skinny skewbald.

"We will ask my sister for a night's lodging," Oliver said as they left the Tower, "and maybe keep Christmas with her household. She is a dear soul. If she can help, then help she will with all her might."

"She might speak for me with the Archbishop . . . ?"

"Bless you," cried Oliver, "it's a very distant connection—her husband is half-brother to the Archbishop's brother-in-law! Even if he were here in England, instead of far away in France, it's doubtful if she's ever spoken to him."

The city was surrounded by open fields that ran beside the river. But Simon hardly saw where they rode, or cared for sights so new and strange to him. His feeling of optimism had gone as suddenly as it had come; he knew only that he had left his brother behind, and that Edmund would move about the country and across the sea as the Court moved, for the King's realms in Europe were vast. What if he had said good-by to his twin forever?

"Take heart, Simon," said Oliver. "Look there at the ice that lies across the fields. Look how the men and lads play there."

Simon looked reluctantly and listlessly where Oliver pointed. All the great flat space that side of the city was flooded by the river and the floods had frozen into sheets of ice. The ice was crowded with truant scholars. They were yelling and shouting as they went about their games—some sliding on polished lanes they had made for themselves, others dragging one another on great lumps of ice. Others again— and these seemed magically skillful—had tied to their feet the blade-bones of oxen and other cattle, and on these they moved at great speed, skimming the surface of the ice like birds. Simon thought what splendor it would be to be sporting there with Edmund, who now seemed utterly lost to him.

"How am I to live?" he cried.

"Hush you," said Oliver, as though Simon were half his years and needed a child's comforting. "You shall see—all will be well for you. I knew it when the steward spoke of your writing, and of the Archbishop of Canterbury. A bishop's household would suit you well, and there are many such. In such a place, your Norman blood would be well fitted."

Simon thought very little of his Norman blood just then. Though it gave him kinship of a sort with the King of England, whose great-grandfather William had crossed the channel from France to conquer and to rule, he would sooner have been an uncouth Englishman with his brother safe at his side.

They had pulled in the horses to watch the games on the ice. The animals puffed and snorted in the cold and their breath rose to mingle with the cloudy breath of their riders. The sun like a red-hot coin was dropping from sight, and they could see the night, a shapeless army whose weapon was snow, moving in from the north to engulf them. They shook up the horses and went on their way, and Simon tried to take an interest in what he saw. The city streets were full of flurry, and beyond the city wall the fine houses of the prosperous merchants and tradesmen stood among winter-shrouded gardens. It took them some time to find the house of Goodman Godfrey, who had married Oliver's sister Joan. Perhaps the directions they were given by passers-by were quite simple to follow, but the speech of the Londoners was strange to ears accustomed to country talk or Norman French.

At last the servant Hodge nosed his lean beast up to Oliver's side.

"Here's the house now, master. A fine courtyard, the last old goody said, and a coat of arms above the door. With a goat and her two kids for a crest, by the looks of it!"

"That's the sign of his trade, Hodge—he's no gentleman bearing his own arms. The Archbishop's sister is Dame Margaret Tanner. Her husband's a leather merchant, as you can tell by his name." Oliver lifted his nose and sniffed. "Pfui! There's leather about, that's certain. There's no mistaking that stench—Goodman Godfrey cures his own hides by the smell of it."

"Shall we knock, then?" Simon asked, cold and stiff and longing to get within doors, never mind whose.

"Beat on the door, Hodge," ordered Oliver. "Let's see if they'll give us a welcome."

The welcome was like a burst of sunshine on that wintry day. They were greeted with incredulous delight, drawn inside to a great fire of huge logs, embraced by Dame Joan. They were entreated by her husband to make themselves at home, they were peered at and giggled at by a number of red-cheeked children who tumbled about the place like a lot of puppies.

"Sit by the fire!" cried one small girl, tugging at Simon's sleeve. "Sit by the fire and tell a tale."

"Elinor, be silent!" her mother ordered. She laughed at Simon. "She is the biggest tease among us. But I daresay you have sisters of your own and know they must be treated most severely."

Simon looked at Dame Joan and shook his head. He smiled at her as he did so, because she was so gay and comfortable, so certain that all was well with the world. But in spite of his smile she must have seen in his eyes that his particular world was upside down. She reached out and took both his hands in hers and pulled him to sit beside her near the fire. Then she looked down at his hands and frowned a little, realizing for the first time that one was whole and one was helpless. She put away the right hand, as though it could very well look after itself, and held only the left, with its limp slack fingers that could not grasp hers. She sat stroking this hand and talking all the time, telling Simon about the children. How Hugh and Roger were the sons of Goodman Godfrey's first wife, rest her soul. And how her own eldest son by her first husband, whose memory she must always cherish, wished to be a goldsmith and seemed likely to do well in the trade. And besides these boys there were Agnes and Alice, there were Randal and Robert and Elinor, and last of all Rose.

"There!" said Dame Joan, in a satisfied way that told Simon his forced smile had become a real one.

Then she sprang up and began bustling about, ordering the kitchen maids and calling for food, carrying in her own hands a great jug of home-brewed ale to pour for her brother and his young companion.

"And now you are here you shall stay for tomorrow's great feast—and for St. Stephen's day, too," she decided. "You see, husband, what a fine fellow my brother is—just as I have always promised you. And this boy, his master's boy—Sir Richard's son—is a boy any mother would be proud of."

"But my brother Edmund is taller and cleverer and has both hands," Simon told her. "And he is to be a page in the King's own household. That is a splendid and a wonderful thing, if you ask me."

As he spoke, the worst of all his sadness was drawn out of him like an arrow from a wound—with pain, but with the promise of clean healing. He thought he had never so quickly felt love and affection for anyone as he felt then for Dame Joan. Because of it he could throw back his shoulders and face anything the world should offer, even though he might have to face it alone.

II

The Archbishop's Kin

SIMON WOULD NOT have believed a few hours
back that he could feel so warm and comfortable
that Christmas Eve. Allowing for the day's abstinence,
they had still eaten well by his standards. Now the

elders among them sat about the bare scrubbed table and talked together. All the children but Hugh and Roger had been bustled off to bed. These two crouched down snugly by the embers at the edge of the fire, making a place there for Simon. The boys did not speak to him much; he seemed to them a complete foreigner. But they looked at him from time to time and smiled, as though to encourage him. And Simon was glad to smile back, soothed by their friendliness and by the warmth of this unfamiliar place.

Gradually he drowsed. He curled up by the hearth with his head on his arm and lay half waking and half sleeping, aware of the flames eating the great logs, of the talk around the table, a steady mumble of unrecognizable words. Then suddenly he was wide awake, for the name of Archbishop Thomas Becket of Canterbury had emerged from that mumble with all the force of a trumpet call.

"Truly I am no more than half-brother to his sister's husband," Goodman Godfrey was saying. "But it is the greatest honor to be related to such a man, however distantly."

"Yet it is a grave thing," said Joan, "that he has fallen foul of the King. Have you heard, brother Oliver, of the King's rages—how he will bellow and tear at his hair, and even roll on the ground, they say, cursing as man never cursed before?" She leaned across the table and said beneath her breath: "He claims descent from the Devil himself!"

The two men exchanged glances and laughed a little, though uneasily.

"And surely," said Joan, "only the Devil's man would so persecute the Lord Archbishop of Canterbury, the Church's very head in England, so that he has been forced to flee from his own people into France for safety."

"Is it true that the Archbishop would not give King Henry his oath of allegiance?" Oliver asked. "We have heard rumors in plenty—but it is difficult to choose which might be the truth."

"It is not true!" his sister cried. "The King has no more faithful subject. But there are certain new laws the King has drawn up, concerning the Church . . . well, you will have heard of all that."

"I know the King would like to meddle in Church appointments—"

"That is a small part of it! Even the law is to be changed. Now if any cleric is to be tried for an offense, the King will have it that he shall be tried by the civil courts—not by ecclesiastics, as it has always been."

"It is a grave business," Goodman Godfrey said. "If the King has his way I believe he will set himself up above the Pope—he has already prevented many churchmen from sending letters to the Holy Father."

"Naturally enough, Archbishop Becket has stood out against these measures," Joan said warmly. "And it is right that he should."

Simon shifted so that he could watch the speakers. The firelight struck upward onto their faces, which had grown serious and earnest as they talked. Dame Joan's gown was of a warm, dark russet cloth, and the white linen veil she wore over her coiled braids made her face look as smooth and as comfortable as a ripe apple. Her husband's long blue tunic, slit at the front, displayed his tawny hose and his pointed shoes of supple leather. Against these colors, subdued but rich, Oliver's sober tunic, stained with travel, showed worn and shabby.

"This is the oath he will not swear then," Oliver was saying. "He will not swear to obey the King in these new commands?"

"He will not swear to observe the new laws, brother, except such as do not injure his duty to God. There are sixteen laws and some are acceptable to any man, of whatever opinion or degree. But for the rest—the Archbishop has said that he will swear *saving the rights of his Order*. Meaning he will always put first his loyalty to God and the Church."

"What has so complicated the business," Goodman Godfrey explained, "is that the other bishops have agreed. And they persuaded the Archbishop, between them, to give his consent to the King's proposals. But when he learned that he must actually sign his name—he would not, he could not for very conscience."

"The laws were written down, then?" Oliver said frowning.

"Ay—drawn up in a great document, to be called the Constitutions. The Constitutions of Clarendon, men call them, since it was at Clarendon castle that the signing took place. Now you know well, brother Oliver, that all laws are not so set down, and that a bad law may thus be changed with time. And so, I do not doubt, the Archbishop believed when he at last agreed to the cajolings of the other bishops. But when he saw that these laws were in fact written— then he withdrew after all. So now the bishops, too, are against him."

"Yet in the old days, when Thomas Becket was Chancellor of England, what friends they were—he and King Henry. I have seen them ride together down Cheapside," Joan told her brother, "and it was pleasure to watch them, they were so merry. The King even sent his eldest son to be educated in the Chancellor's household."

"In those days," said Oliver, "he was not an ordained priest. Is it this that has changed him?"

"He was in minor orders," Joan replied. "A deacon, I think. Yet it is a strange thing that for all the magnificence of his household, he himself lived sparely. Truly he dressed as a rich lord would. But though any who pleased might eat and drink at his table, and do so splendidly, he touched no wine and ate very little. Nor did any woman ever enter his life— even his worst enemy must testify to this."

"The King thought to have an easy tool, perhaps, once the Chancellor became the Archbishop."

"That is plain to see!" she exclaimed. "But he warned the King—did he not, husband? Was not King Henry warned of what might follow if he forced the Chancellor to become Archbishop of Canterbury? 'If you do this thing, my liege,' said Thomas Becket himself when he learned what was afoot, 'then you will rue it.' It was so, was it not, husband?"

"Some such words," he agreed. "And they are bitterly fulfilled."

Simon lay quietly, wide awake now and listening intently. Dame Joan was telling her brother stories that she clearly loved to recount. Her husband's connection with the Archbishop of Canterbury, slight though it was, filled her with pride and pleasure, and she liked nothing better than to speak of the great man whose present difficulties were a matter of such concern. Like many another Londoner, too, she rejoiced in the fact that the Archbishop had been born in the city, the son of a merchant who had come from Normandy to settle and trade in London. Gilbert Becket had done well in the city of his adoption, and because of a dream his wife had had at the child's birth, he accepted from the start that his son Thomas was destined for great things.

"As was soon proved true," said Dame Joan. "And when he was a scholar at Merton Priory, I have heard, it was plain that he was apart from the rest. He could not fail to make his mark in this world— as he shall no doubt in the next. Ever since he was made Chancellor because of his wit and wisdom, men have spoken of him with awe and envy. . . ." She broke off and held up her hand, forgetting her story. "Listen! One of the children is crying." She rose at once and went swiftly away from them to the child's bedside.

Simon shifted from his place on the hearth. He leaned on the table beside Goodman Godfrey.

"Where is the Archbishop now, sir?"

Godfrey smiled at the boy. "I thought you were asleep down there. Listen to my two urchins snoring! The Archbishop is at Pontigny in France, Simon, at the Cistercian Abbey there."

"I still do not understand why he went there," Simon said. "Did the King threaten his life?"

"As nearly as he dared, though not in so many words. When Thomas Becket was Chancellor, he spent vast sums of money on the King's behalf. Suddenly the King demanded repayment, swearing that the Archbishop had seized the money for himself. . . . He did right to go away."

"He is a brave man," Oliver said, shaking his head. "But he suffers for his bravery. It is a bitter thing that he has fled into France."

"It was the only course open to him. The King had forbidden all correspondence with the Pope. From France, the Archbishop may address himself to the Holy Father without fear."

"If he had been still at Canterbury," Simon said, "would he have given me a place, do you suppose?"

"It is very likely," Godfrey assured him. "And he will return, Simon—no doubt of that. It seems to me best, though Oliver must be on his way, that you should remain here with us. Then when the Archbishop comes back to England I shall go to his sister and ask her to speak for you."

Immense comfort filled Simon. He could not speak his gratitude, but only smiled. A splendid dream filled his mind. . . . The King and the Archbishop would make up their quarrel . . . they would visit one an-

other, attended by their servants and gentleman attendants . . . the best page in the King's household
and the indispensable scribe from the Archbishop's
establishment would meet frequently . . . the brothers
would be together again. . . .

Dame Joan came back into the room.

"Now let us be silent together," she said. "It is
barely two hours to midnight and the birth of Our
Lord. Rest quietly."

As silence settled over them, Simon tried to medi-
tate as he had been told, but he had constantly to
snatch his thoughts back from the events of the day
and the hopes of the future.

At last it was time to go to church. They muffled
themselves against the bitter night and prepared to
leave the house. Dame Joan stopped Simon on the
threshold and pulled his cloak closer about his throat,
as though he had become already one more child of
her large family.

"In the morning we will send to tell your brother
where you are lodged," she promised.

The snow that had threatened to fall at dusk hung
still on the horizon. Bright sharp frost made the
cobbles treacherous. With two servants ahead and
two behind carrying flaming torches, they set out
among all their neighbors to hear their Christmas-
tide mass at midnight in the parish church.

It was two days after Christmas that Simon heard
Dame Joan calling him to come quickly into the hall.
There he found Edmund, wearing the King's livery,

grinning with pride of himself and pleasure at seeing his brother again so soon.

"I have no duties until sundown. So I have come at once to see how you are getting on here."

"How fine you look!" cried Simon. "That tunic's made of better cloth than I ever saw—and that's a jewel in your cap, brother!"

"It is a bauble, no more," replied Edmund casually, spinning the cap in his hand. It was clear that three days in his new surroundings had already made him a man of the world. "But you, Simon—you, too, look twice yourself. You have a fine color in your cheeks. And that is a neat little dagger you wear in your belt. I never saw that before."

"Goodman Godfrey gave it to me. It was a Christmas token. This is a splendid household, Edmund— it may not be the King's, but it is full of friends. Do you know that Goodman Godfrey is half-brother to the husband of the sister of the Archbishop of Canterbury?"

Edmund frowned. The business he had heard most talked about, he said, was the quarrel between the King and the Archbishop.

"The King and all the bishops are conferring at Marlborough. None knows what may happen. They say the King is in a greater fury than ever. He has learned that the King of France has helped the Archbishop in his exile—has given him hospitality and sympathy and treated him with great honor. He may even speak for the Archbishop with the Pope. It is a business of great importance, I can tell you."

"Don't look so solemn," Simon protested. "You may be a page wearing the King's livery but you need not bother yourself yet with affairs of state!"

That made Edmund hurl his cap at Simon. They fell into a wild but friendly scuffle, in which Simon easily made up for a limp hand by his nimbleness in twisting and turning.

But there was too much to talk about for them to waste time in wrangling. Simon had to hear about Edmund's new situation in life, about the other pages and household attendants who had remained in London while the court moved to Marlborough; and about the duties he had to learn.

"It is much as it was in our grandfather's hall—but grander. Where one page would hold the ewer and the basin for handwashing, with a napkin over his arm for drying—here there are three of us: one with the ewer, one with the basin, one with the napkin."

When Oliver came in, he looked at Edmund with great satisfaction.

"You have found the place that was meant for you. Already you have grown confident and you hold your head high. I shall leave all the happier for having seen you today."

A silence fell on them. The boys knew that Oliver must go, for he had his living to make. But the thought of separation from this last familiar friend kept them tongue-tied. For the first time Oliver admitted that he was going overseas to the Low Countries, where he had spent some time as a young man. Hodge would go with him.

"Who knows, I may find a way to riches. Then I shall return and seek you."

The brothers rode with Oliver to the bank of the Thames and watched him and Hodge taken off to their ship that swung at anchor in midstream, straining at her gear as the full tide took her and bent her toward the promise of the ocean. Gulls wheeled and screamed above her, and a long halloo of greeting rang across the water as the small boat reached her side.

In silence Edmund and Simon returned the way they had come. It was a very solemn moment. All their childhood now lay behind them. They were alone and must do the best they could for themselves.

"I'll not come indoors again," Edmund said, breaking the long silence as they came within sight of Goodman Godfrey's house. "It is my first time out and I had best be punctual. But there will be other times. All the while you are with Dame Joan it is no more than a few minutes' ride to visit you."

"And all the while you are at the Tower," said Simon, "but that will not be always."

"We must manage," replied Edmund, firmly.

It seemed almost as though Edmund had become an older brother, sensible and courageous and greatly to be admired. Simon felt that he could never match Edmund in these virtues. He could only hope to find a place for himself where he might be quietly useful. It was great good fortune that during the year in his grandfather's castle he had learned from the chaplain to write with a skill and firmness far beyond his years; and he had learned how to read and calculate numbers of a simple sort. He might never have had the patience if his useless hand had not kept him from climbing and hunting and pursuits of that kind. Once again he felt that his father had made him a parting gift of priceless value.

Dame Joan was looking for Simon when he came in from watching Edmund ride away.

"My husband has been speaking of your future, Simon. Shall we go and hear what he has to say?"

Godfrey was standing at the high table in his countinghouse where all the money business of his trade was done. A couple of lads were counting and weighing a great pile of hides. Along the back of the table, which was placed against the wall, small plump moneybags, tied at the mouth, suggested that this merchant of leather was in a very good way of business. Today he wore a long gown in the fashionable green-blue called watchet, with fur at the neck, almost like a gentleman. He had been that afternoon discussing city affairs with the sheriff and the portreeves, or magistrates, and so he had put on his best.

"I have been hearing from my brother-in-law Oliver about your scholarship, Simon—how you can read and write and know the uses of the calculus. I know you have a worthy ambition to serve the Archbishop of Canterbury. But I hear more and more of the King's anger and threats. God alone knows when Thomas Becket will return to Canterbury. I have undertaken to care for you until you are settled. Might you not work here in the countinghouse keeping a tally of my trade and all that concerns it? What do you say?"

Simon's hesitation was so slight it was not noticed. It was the hesitation that came from knowing that his proud brother Edmund would have something to say about Norman blood, a London tradesman and the strict rules of family honor . . . well, he would deal with that—and firmly—when the time came. Meanwhile, he was certainly old enough to make up his mind.

"I say—with all my heart!" he cried. "And so I may work for my keep, and not be a burden on your household."

"God bless you, Simon!" said Dame Joan. "Now you are one of us—you are another son of the house! And when the time comes for your cause to be spoken of to the Archbishop—why, it will be like one of his own kin coming to him." She threw her arms round him and hugged him warmly. "Never forget that when he was a young man the Archbishop himself worked in such a way—in the countinghouse of his father, Gilbert Becket, a merchant like my good husband."

Godfrey was laughing at her vehemence. "Archbishop Thomas should be told what a champion he has in you, wife."

"Simon shall tell him when the time comes," she retorted.

As she spoke, they heard someone running along the paved passageway from the street. The heavy door was flung open and Hugh burst into the room. He must have run hard and fast—he was breathless and white.

"I have heard something terrible! Oh, Father—!"

"The children?" cried his mother. "Is one of the children hurt?"

Hugh shook his head. "No—no . . ."

"What is it, Hugh?" his father asked. "Get your breath back, boy. Steady, now, and tell us."

"The watch is crying a proclamation of the King," Hugh managed to get out. "They cried it first on Tower Hill, and then in the Minories—and now they are bent this way. It is a proclamation against all the clerks and kin of Archbishop Thomas Becket of Canterbury! But we are not his kin, father, are we? Not truly his kin. . . ."

"We have always been proud of it," replied Godfrey. "Let us be proud of it now."

"God save us!" Dame Joan cried. "What have we done that the King should name us in the street?"

"Listen!" Simon caught at her arm.

Far away, they heard the marching of a dozen or so men. Then came the sharp clank of pike ends on cobbles and a voice, distantly crying. In the counting-house they stood, the four of them, straining their ears, unable to make out any word, knowing only by its rhythm the familiar "God Save the King" with which each crying concluded. Then again came the sound of marching, moving away to the west, to call at the next vantage point.

For a second or two the silence held. Then came more feet running, lighter and swifter—the feet of neighbors hurrying to the house of Goodman Godfrey, to beat upon his door and shout to him a warning of what the King had commanded.

III

What the King Commanded . . .

THIS WAS WHAT the King's men had proclaimed in the streets of London: that all the kin of Archbishop Thomas Becket, of whatever degree, should be banished and sent to join him in exile. Likewise

27

all those priests and clerks in any way connected with him, and their families down to their nephews and nieces, while all their goods and chattels would be confiscated by the King. And with a final touch of savagery, the King chose Ranulph de Broc, a most bitter enemy to the Archbishop, to see the sentence carried out.

Terrible confusion had followed the proclamation. Simon was unable now to recall the ordered course of events, for everything seemed to happen at once. On the warning of their neighbors, Godfrey and his wife had gathered together the children and what belongings they could conveniently bundle, and they had thought to escape to Goodman Godfrey's sister, some miles out of London. But there was no time. Remotely related to the Archbishop as they were, the King's warrant was served on them before they were able to leave. They were escorted to Lambeth Palace, where they were obliged by command of the King to take an oath that they would present themselves to Archbishop Thomas as soon as they reached France. Then at once the journey began.

They were soon joined by many more, families or single individuals, cleric and lay, poorly equipped for travel; and at various stages along the road the crowd multiplied and the confusion increased in proportion. There were old people who dropped behind and who had to be left with whoever would take them in to die; and it was clear that many of the smallest children would not see the end of the journey.

Soon there were more than a hundred people being

driven to the coast, then two hundred, then three. The final tally was something like four hundred souls. Many of them, like Simon, had been caught up in the hurly-burly by chance and now could not escape.

The last Simon saw of Dame Joan and the youngest children was when they were hustled along with fifty or so more into the shelter of a barn for the night while he and Hugh and Roger were obliged to continue to the next village. Of Goodman Godfrey there was by then no sign; he had fallen back some miles earlier, when one of the smaller boys wrenched his ankle.

All along the road, people came from their homes to know the cause of the disturbance. Learning what was happening to these unfortunate souls, many tried to help them, offering food and shelter for the night. The better-placed travelers, who had money for bargaining, contrived in one or two cases to get hold of a lean horse or mule or donkey. Some of the prosperous citizens in the towns the column passed through might have done more, but they were wary of the King's displeasure. The poor, for whom Archbishop Thomas had come to stand as a symbol of strength against tyranny, had none the less to consider their own situation. Many wept that they had no more to offer.

Although they had become separated from the rest of the family, Simon and Hugh and Roger contrived for some time to remain together. In the long nightmare of the journey from London to the coast, in the confusion of the increasing crowd of travelers, and the way they were herded and harried, few groups remained unbroken. Not the least of the horrors was the constant distraught inquiry of parents seeking children, husbands seeking wives. It was in this way that Simon and Hugh lost Roger, for he darted off to ask a crowd of strangers if they had seen his parents, and was hurried off with them to a different point of embarkation.

Hugh was still at Simon's side when they reached the coast. By this time, too, they had fallen in with Brother Oswin, a middle-aged monk who was by nature a leader, and to whom, therefore, all his group of travelers looked for guidance. It was because Brother Oswin gave Simon a hand aboard that he was parted from Hugh. One of the men-at-arms bundled him away to the next boat. He shouted and kicked and struggled, but the man, laughing, held him all the harder.

"You will meet in France," Brother Oswin said. He held Simon as firmly as Hugh had been held, for he feared the boy might try to scramble overboard.

Simon shook his head. He gave up the struggle. "No," he said. "No, we shall never meet again. I shall never see any of them again—never—never. . . ."

His teeth chattered with cold and misery. Sheer fatigue made him sob, and he beat feebly with his one good fist against Brother Oswin's broad chest.

Close by, an old man was standing, muttering over and over again: "It is God's will. It is God's will that I go. God wills that I die far from home."

"King Henry wills it!" retorted Brother Oswin. He was a short square man with a red face that grew redder when he was angry—then even his tonsured crown, with its fringe of gray curly hair, became scarlet as a cock's comb with indignation.

"Ay—the King wills it—the King wills our misery!" repeated another man nearby. The cry was taken up. A great and furious muttering ran among those aboard. "The King—the King wills our misery as he wills that of the Lord Archbishop!"

Brother Oswin tried to comfort Simon. He pulled the boy within the shelter of his rough cloak and rubbed him hard between the shoulder blades to warm him.

"Here," he said, moving toward the stern, "if we crouch among these bales we shall be sheltered from the weather a little. God save us all, it seems a mighty small boat for the journey. Leave off your grief, Simon, and ask St. Peter to intercede for us. We need the help of a good boatman."

Everyone on board seemed old and worn-out. There was no one of Simon's age; he was a child among grandparents. A fog lay across the channel, blown by a freakish wind that barely filled sail enough to draw them. For a time the several boats hallooed to one another at intervals. Then the fog increased. A muffling silence settled on the water and the sail grew limp.

Brother Oswin had bread and meat in a cloth and shared what he had with Simon. The meat was tough and rank, for this was midwinter and the supplies of those who had little to hoard were running out. But the bread was fresh and good.

"I pawned my leather belt in the last village and the fellow gave good value. A twist of rope does well enough to keep my gown tidy."

Brother Oswin sounded very cheerful, and Simon tried to respond to his tone. He knew the monk had little to be cheerful about. He had had a dispensation to visit his sick brother who was priest of a parish attached to the Archbishopric of Canterbury. When the warrant came, it had seemed to Brother Oswin that the only way to save the sick man's life was to take his place without consulting him.

"I was glad enough to fool Ranulph de Broc's men," he admitted, chuckling. "I have as little connection with the Archbishop as you yourself, my poor lad. But let us find honor in being named his men by no less than the King of England!"

Simon gave him a rather wan smile. He knew he had found a sturdy friend in Brother Oswin. But at that moment he would have traded him gladly for the London family he had thought to make his own. As for Edmund, his dear twin, he had not courage even to think of him. It was not in this manner that he had supposed he would seek out the Archbishop of Canterbury.

As the dark came down, the fog parted before a stiffer breeze. The sail flapped heavily and lazily—then cracked as the wind suddenly filled it. The sailors shouted, the helmsman called for a sounding. In the very last gleam of daylight they saw the coast ahead.

The fresh wind that had promised them a haven died as quickly as it had been born. Again the fog engulfed them. They lay all night offshore and it was not until long past noon of the next day that they reached land, cold and hungry, yet so relieved at feeling the firm ground beneath them that they were almost happy. The ship turned for home at once, they were abandoned in a foreign land—but anything seemed better than what had gone before.

Now they must seek out the Archbishop, as they had been forced to swear. Few of these simple souls had realized how far from the coast was the Cistercian Abbey of Pontigny, where the Archbishop had found refuge. They had supposed that once they reached France their troubles would be ended. When they learned the truth, many of them threw themselves down on the frozen ground and declared they would go no further, they would rather die there where they lay.

Brother Oswin's rage was splendid to see.

"Rouse up, you cowards! Have you never heard of the sin of despair? If any among you dare not face the journey, let him consider that an oath under duress may be absolved. Think deeply, however, before you release yourselves. What living can there be for you in this place?"

As he spoke, two men and some boys came running over the brow of the hill. Mostly the fugitives were English born, but there were enough among them who spoke the Norman French that had come to England with the Conqueror. Therefore they were

able to make themselves understood, and to understand what was being said, though the peasant dia-
lect of the newcomers did not help.

"Already others of your sort have passed this way,"
one man told them, "and we have heard how the King
of England persecutes the great Archbishop's kin."

"We are farmers," said the second, "and this is a
lean time of year. But between us we have bread
enough to feed you at least for today. When our
good King Louis hears of this, he will repay us. He
is a good man and the friend of poor exiles."

"I have a barn where you may shelter till daybreak," the first man went on. He called up two of
the boys. "Gil, lead the way. Thibault, run ahead and
warn your mother to bake more bread—do not listen to her protests. Spread straw for beds. It is the
least we may do."

This kindness roused the fugitives. They went gladly
after young Gil and soon found themselves in shelter. There was hay and straw in the barn; the stalled
beasts at one end made a little warmth. The family
living quarters were built on to one side of the barn
and it was not long before someone discovered that
wall was warm. It was so much better than the open
field they had feared that their spirits rose, and they
began almost to boast of the terrible experiences
they had shared during the past days.

"At the end of the first day my feet were bleeding—I had to wrap them in rags."

"Ah, but what of Friar Wulfram and his two old
sisters—we shall not see them again!"

"There was a poor soul with a baby at her breast, and the child was already dead of cold. . . ."

And so it went on.

Brother Oswin made a place in the straw for Simon and told him to rest quietly until he returned. It seemed a long time before he came back, but when he reappeared he had foraged a piece of sausage, eight hen's eggs, and a loaf of bread. He gave away four of the eggs and half the loaf. The rest he shared with the boy, whom he now looked upon as his charge.

"Before I was a monk I was a soldier," he explained. "A soldier always knows where to go for food." His small, blue eyes suddenly twinkled with merriment. "In those days I bought my goods with kisses from the farmer's wife and daughters. Now I offer them my prayers. God bless them, they have gentle hearts and a great regard for charity."

"Tell me about when you were a soldier," Simon said, roused at last from his woes.

"It was when King Henry went to fight for Toulouse. Some said it was a false claim he fought for, but he fought all the same. And with him went his great Chancellor—"

"And I know who that was," cried Simon. "It was Thomas Becket, who has become the Lord Archbishop of Canterbury—whose kin we are—or so King Henry says."

"Ay, it was the same. And I wish I might give you a true notion of his splendor. Seven hundred knights were in his household. During the war he maintained twelve hundred more, with four thousand serving-men besides. To each knight he gave three shillings a day toward the cost of his horses and his esquires. And every knight dined at the Chancellor's own table."

"And did the Chancellor himself go into battle? Dame Joan told me he was already a deacon—could he fight, then?"

"Well," said Brother Oswin, "great men have great ways. At that time he put off the clerk and became a soldier." There was a reminiscent gleam in Brother Oswin's eye. He sat beside Simon in the straw with his gown hitched up over his hairy calves. His sandaled feet, the big toes curled and aggressive, though they were blue with cold gave an impression of immense sturdiness. It was not difficult to imagine the fighting man he had once been. "The Chancellor was a great chancellor, and he was a great knight. Now he is a great churchman—the greatest of our day, I faithfully believe. God keep him, and restore him where he belongs."

"Amen," said Simon. He was filled with the sudden glowing realization that of all of them there, only he had any true business with the Archbishop, being bent on becoming his servant. "Go on," he said softly.

Then Brother Oswin told how Thomas Becket, Chancellor of England, had ridden against a most famous French knight, Engelram de Trie, and un-horsed him. . . . How for his dauntless ways and his splendor and his chivalry all men had honored him, not least his enemies in the field. . . .

Brother Oswin suddenly passed both hands over his face and said in a troubled voice, "I should not think of these things now. Like him, I have vowed myself to another Master and fight in a different battle. . . ."

"You have told a fine tale," Simon said, his eyes glowing.

"And the last for tonight! One day I will tell you how he went as the King's ambassador to France, with two hundred knights in his train, with twenty-four suits of raiment to wear once and give away, with horses and sumpter mules and baggage carts, and his own private chapel with vessels of gold and silver, hangings of silk and velvet. Monkeys rode the mules, and footboys went ahead singing as they entered each village their own English songs. . . . Now say your prayers, my boy, and I will settle to my office."

Deep darkness and quiet soon came down upon the crowded barn. The exiles slept in exhaustion. Sometimes one or another would cry out in his dreams. But mostly the only sound was the shifting of the cattle and their sudden stamping on the beaten earth floor, and the harsh grating of their rough pelts as they rubbed themselves on the wooden sides and heads of their stalls.

In the days that followed the weather improved. It was bitterly cold, but without wind or snow, and the sun shone at midday in a clear sky. The exiles made their way as best they could, begging food and shelter.

Since their tale was increasingly known, they seldom lacked either, however poor it might be. As they went through various towns, some of them decided they would seek absolution from their forced vow to the King and stay behind to find a living for themselves.

And now those who continued began to speak of what was ahead. They began to speculate upon their arrival before the Archbishop. For the first time they talked less of themselves and their plight than of him they were sworn to seek out. Not all of them even knew him, so wide and unscrupulous was the King's mandate. But others had been his clerks or his servingmen, or were related to him by marriage— like Goodman Godfrey. Some had known him when he was still a young man uncertain of his future. Many had tales to tell.

"You may know his greatness by his stature—he is a head taller than any other man in England."

"No man has a keener eye for a hawk or a horse."

"Some say he should give in to the King and accept what he demands—"

"Ah, some do say indeed that Archbishop Becket is an obstinate man and proud."

"He is a different man from him you knew as Chancellor."

"I remember him when he was a child," said one old woman, a hardy, cheerful creature who had stood the journey far better than many of the men. "His mother always knew he was destined for great things in the Church. She had prophetic dreams when he was born."

"And his father also knew," said another woman. "For when he took young Thomas to be educated at the Priory of Merton, he bowed to his son in parting, and the Prior was greatly scandalized. 'I know what I do,' said Gilbert Becket. 'That boy will be great in the sight of the Lord.'"

So it went on, tale after tale. As the days passed, and the weary miles from the coast to Pontigny, the feeling of suspense and excitement grew among them. In Simon it was like a second heart beating. When he considered how he had come here with the rest, it was as though he had been helped miraculously to what he most desired. Though he had never seen the Archbishop, it seemed to him that he knew him well.

At last they came near the end of their journey. Barely ten miles now separated them from Pontigny. If all went well, that day would see the end of their weary travels.

Within an hour they had overtaken two other small parties from England. They had landed on a different coast and taken another road. Simon ran among them, eagerly seeking news of the family he had lost.

"There was none like them in our boat," he was told every time.

"I should have noticed a lot of children," said one woman bitterly. "Have I not lost my own?"

At last they saw ahead of them in the dusk the abbey buildings, with the great church, towerless and still unfinished, rising up among them. Before the gates of the monastery a number of people were waiting, and others were converging upon the same point. Most carried bundles and leaned upon staves. All looked weary, yet still they seemed to have an air of expectation, for the last hard steps were lightened by realization of the goal ahead.

As though by common consent, each little knot of two or three arriving at the gate waited to be overtaken by the next. When at last it seemed as though all who were likely to come at that time had arrived, it was agreed that they should announce their arrival by pulling the bell rope. But then, for some reason of diffidence or fear, none was found willing to take this step. They hung back and argued among themselves.

Brother Oswin, Simon at his elbow, began pushing and shouldering his way among the fifty or so men and women gathered about the gate.

"What is the delay?" he demanded.

"Brother, we hesitate to ring the bell," said a man at the head of the crowd. "It seems to us an unmannerly thing, now that we are here by the King's command, to force ourselves on the Archbishop. What are we to say to him? How tell our story?"

"Do you agree that I shall be your spokesman?" Brother Oswin demanded in his blunt way.

There were murmurs of agreement and a few of dissent. But Brother Oswin would not stay to argue. He seized the knot of the bell rope in his square, capable hand and gave it a good tug.

As the bell pealed above their heads, an uneasy silence settled on the crowd. They waited restlessly for the door to open. Perhaps Simon was not the only one who half expected it would swing back to reveal the great Archbishop Thomas Becket of Canterbury, splendidly clad in cope and miter, with his great cross borne above him. . . .

But it was the porter who opened to them—a small thin monk with a worried face and a bunch of keys that seemed almost too heavy for him to carry.

"God save us all!" he cried when he saw them. "More of you? Why do you come here, day after day? Is it to kill your Archbishop with sorrow and pity?"

"We are here to keep our oath to the King of England," said Brother Oswin, shortly. "We do not come of our free will. I pray you, brother, go to the Archbishop and tell him we have come."

"He is at vespers with the rest of the community," replied the porter. "You must wait in the cloister."

He stood back and let them by. They passed him rather nervously. The men snatched at their caps and the women bowed their heads as they entered the abbey precincts.

As they stood there waiting among the increasing shadows, they heard the monks singing from the church close by. Then the singing ended. With it ended, also, the whispering and shuffling of the exiles. A deep, expectant silence settled over them. In the silence came the sound of the monks emerging from the church, their sandals tapping and grating on the pavements, their gowns and girdles swishing.

They came in procession along the cloister. At their head walked the Abbot. Behind came a second procession, the novices led by the Precentor.

Passing toward the south cloister, the Abbot became aware for the first time of the crowd waiting silently. He held up his hand and all behind him shuffled to a standstill.

"There's the Archbishop!" Simon said to Brother Oswin. "I knew him at once!"

He had spoken, though impulsively, in a whisper. Because he chose the moment when every monk had come to a standstill, and because in that enclosed space each sound was magnified, his words echoed as though he had shouted them.

As Simon felt his face flame in confusion, the monk walking on the Abbot's right hand stepped a little forward. It was as though he had answered a summons. He was very tall, very straight, intensely pale. His eyes, so dark with compassion that they looked almost black, seemed to burn in the dusk of the cloister, easily piercing its increasing shadows.

He moved a pace or two toward the exiles as they stood huddled uneasily together, a mob of strangers who had never been so far from home. He stretched out his hands—then let them fall helplessly to his side.

Movement began among the crowd and some stepped forward eagerly, or some went down on their knees, or some covered their faces as though they could not bear to see the anguish in his.

They murmured, one after the other, "My lord . . .

Lord Thomas . . . Good Lord Archbishop . . . Your Grace. . . ."

The Archbishop's gaze seemed piercingly centered on the boy who had first spoken, as though he needed some focus in all this crowd of upturned faces. Brother Oswin gave Simon the least shove forward.

Without taking his eyes from the Archbishop's drawn face, Simon fell on both knees.

"Father," he said. . . .

IV

Pontigny, 1166

AT A HIGH DESK under the thin, tall window,
Simon, his sandaled feet curled round the rungs
of a stool, was copying a letter. There were five men
in the room, ignoring him, busy about their own

urgent conversation. Simon knew them all by now, friends and disciples of the Archbishop who had followed him into exile, men of stature and spirit and learning. At first he had been awed by them; now he was at ease among them.

"It is all very well to counsel humility and moderation," Herbert of Bosham was saying. "What does King Henry know of such virtues? No—since words have failed, the time has come for some kind of action. I have told the Archbishop so."

William Fitzstephen raised his eyebrows slightly. Clerk, chaplain, friend to Thomas Becket, with a precise manner, he resented so robust an approach to delicate problems. "Was that your place, Master Herbert?" he said.

"For that matter, what is his place—any more than yours or mine?" demanded Llewellyn the Welshman. He was official crossbearer to the Archbishop and so inclined to think himself privileged. Like others of his countrymen, he was a blunt man impatient of gentleness. If anyone was to make a straightforward remark to Thomas Becket, then Llewellyn the Welshman considered it should be he. His frankness could make Herbert of Bosham shudder in his turn.

"Here, the Archbishop is a simple monk," said his confessor, Robert of Merton, who had known him longer than any of them. "He is a member of the community, no more, no less. He is strengthened in consequence."

"Strengthened in spirit, yes," agreed Herbert. "But this exile *must* be ended. No doubt the King does very well with an empty see at Canterbury. But it cannot remain empty. It is already a year and a half since we left England. What is to become of those poor souls left without a pastor?"

"Is it only a year and a half?" The fifth man, John of Salisbury, sighed as he spoke. He was standing near Simon at the window, and he looked out over the deep stone sill with an expression of intense longing, as though he saw all England lying there, but out of reach.

Herbert of Bosham was pacing the room impatiently. This was his own lodging and he had invited the other four to speak with him here because he had believed he might influence them. He was the most militant and spirited of those who had followed Thomas Becket into exile. He detested his master's humiliation and longed only to see him restored to his rightful place. He was convinced that the King should be challenged and a reconciliation somehow brought about.

He paused by Simon and looked over his shoulder.

"Have you finished yet?"

"A few more words, sire," Simon mumbled, aware that he would have finished by now had he not allowed himself to be distracted by the talk.

The year was moving toward the spring, the second spring that Simon had seen at Pontigny. The rest of the fugitives had gone on their way, but he had been taken into the Archbishop's service as he had known from the outset he would be. At first he had been put to lessons with the scholars who had come to the abbey for their education. Simon was far in advance of the rest, thanks to his grandfather's chaplain. After some months, though he shared the scholars' quarters and their organized sports and pastimes, he had been made Master Herbert's charge. He was page, secretary, general factotum.

Herbert of Bosham was a vigorous, handsome man. He was, as John of Salisbury had been known to remark, more warrior than priest, though he had considerable learning. He was the friend and master Simon needed. Ever since the death of his parents the boy had been losing those he loved. He had been separated from Edmund, from Oliver, from Goodman Godfrey's family, now far away in Italy; and then from Brother Oswin, who had left Pontigny to seek and join a monastery of his own Order until it was safe to return to England.

In the first months at Pontigny, Simon had been unhappy, rebellious, full of suspicions and doubts. Though he had reached the place he wanted, he could not enjoy it. He had imagined himself especially marked by the Archbishop—as though because he had chosen Thomas Becket, Thomas Becket must also have marked and chosen him. But he seldom saw the Archbishop, and although at that first encounter there had appeared so sharp and deep a sympathy between them, it seemed soon forgotten.

Then on Shrove Tuesday Simon had gone with the rest of the scholars to make his confession. The moment he knelt down he realized that the cowled

figure sitting quietly in the dimly lit chapter house
was Archbishop Thomas himself. No one else was so
tall and spare or had such a forcefully long and jut-
ting nose.

"Bless me, father," Simon mumbled. Then the word
father released in him such a flood of memory and
misery that he could not speak. Tears filled his eyes,
his throat felt hot and twice its size. He struggled to
control himself, but he could not. He put his hand
over his eyes and sobbed.

The quiet aloofness of the confessor left the Archbishop. He turned toward Simon, and leaning forward compassionately, he took the boy's limp left hand
and held it—not, as Dame Joan had held it, tenderly,
but so firmly that it seemed as though he would force
into it a little of his own enormous strength. He spoke
gently and quietly, and although Simon barely heard
the words, the rich voice gradually laid itself like a
balm on his unhappiness. His tears ceased, they were
dried by the warmth and sympathy that were offered
him. He lifted his head and looked into the pale face,
with its large imperious nose and intense eyes, and
his own troubles then seemed so insignificant, so utterly without meaning that he was ashamed.

Later, when Simon's confession was done and he
had rid his conscience of what were almost all sins
of rebellion, the Archbishop blessed him and then
held out his hand. He was smiling for the first time,
not sadly, but with a firm and even humorous encouragement. Simon bent and kissed the hand held
out to him.

"Go in peace, my child," said Archbishop Thomas. "Pray for me."

If his surroundings had been only a little different, Simon would have skipped his way back to his companions, his heart felt so light and joyful.

"Your turn," he whispered to Eustace, one of the scholars, the next in the row of kneeling, fidgety boys.

"About time," grumbled Eustace. "You've been long enough to confess every sin in the calendar!"

Simon smiled. He sank comfortably on his knees and considered his modest penance.

From that time, though he saw Thomas Becket rarely, Simon knew that he was not forgotten. Sometimes the Archbishop would ask for him specially to serve an early mass. Once, when Simon was shivering in his bed with a feverish chill, the infirmarian, Brother Piers, came in at supper time with a bowl of soup that he carried with exaggerated care.

"This comes to you from the Archbishop's own table. Master Herbert told him of your sickness, it seems. Who would have thought," said Brother Piers, sounding a shade disgruntled, "that his lordship would have time to consider a skinny brat of your sort?"

"It is because he has been sick himself so often, I daresay," replied Simon.

Indeed the Archbishop's health had caused great concern. The Pope himself had blessed and sent him a habit of the Order, that he might feel himself a true member of the community at Pontigny. Therefore, he had tried to follow the rule in all things. This was more rigorous even than his usual custom and he had made himself seriously ill. And being so low in health he had also suffered greatly from an abscess in his mouth, which was relieved only when he had two teeth drawn.

However that might be, the soup warmed Simon in more than his body. Brother Piers stood watching him as he sat with his hands round the bowl. Though the infirmarian had a gruff manner at times, he was truly devoted to the care of the sick. Two nights before, when Simon had wakened sweating and crying out in a fearful dream, Brother Piers had soothed him tenderly and firmly. In his dream, Simon had been lying with his father's cold hand clasping his, and try as he would he could not free himself. . . .

As Simon's pen moved slowly and carefully over the last few words of the letter he was copying, he heard Herbert of Bosham say something about the King. Remote though it might be, talk of the King's court filled Simon with excitement, for it was his sole link now with his brother Edmund.

"The news is that the King will hold court at Angers this Easter. May not the Archbishop be reminded of this, Master John? And might not two or three reasonable men among us seek him out there?"

Simon nearly dropped his pen. Excitement jerked his elbow, his slack hand swept against the inkhorn slung round his neck, the ink spilled over his gown, and he cried out in annoyance at his carelessness.

"What's the matter with the boy?" John of Salisbury asked.

"The ink!" cried Simon, rubbing furiously at the spots on his gown.

"The sign of a scholar," William Fitzstephen told him.

"And when these reasonable men reach the King," said Llewellyn the Crossbearer, ignoring the interruption, "what are they to say to him? Do they beg permission to go home—where they are forbidden even to correspond with the Holy Father? It is not to be thought of!"

"If one among us might return to England it would mean a steppingstone between Pontigny and Canterbury—between the King and the Pope and the Archbishop," William Fitzstephen said, reasonably.

"Well, it can be discussed later," said Herbert of Bosham. "We will speak of it another time."

With that the meeting broke up and no one was left but Master Herbert, and Simon still scrubbing at the inkspots.

"How did you come to spill the ink, boy?"

"I heard you speak of King Henry and his court. . . . Sir—if you should indeed go to Angers, I beg you to take me with you as your servant. My brother is there, sir—have you forgotten? Edmund, my twin, who is a page to the King. If I could only see him. . . ."

"Bless you, I had forgotten Edmund. Well, if the matter reaches any conclusion I see no reason why you should not come. But there is much work to be done first. Archbishop Thomas is not easily swayed."

Simon knew that well enough. Indeed there was very little he did not know about this affair by now. Everyone had a tale to tell, everyone took sides. And Simon, like others employed on letter writing, had confidential knowledge, too. He knew much of what had passed between the Archbishop and the English bishops, between the Archbishop and the Pope. He knew that there were many who blamed the Archbishop for his flight, declaring that he should have remained in England to fight it out to the last among his own people. Others recognized him as their bastion against tyranny, the only hope of the Church in England that was threatened with separation from Rome. And besides these were his true disciples, who would stand by him through every storm—who would suffer exile and even death with him cheerfully, so they believed.

At night in the scholars' dormitory, Simon now lay awake often, thinking of Edmund and the sudden chance that he might see him again. How much would he have grown? Even six months made a difference to boys of their age, and by the time the brothers met, if indeed Master Herbert's plan should bear fruit, it would be nearer eighteen months since their parting. Simon had had no news at all of his brother all that long time.

It was the hardest parting and the most complete. A few months after he was settled at Pontigny, he had heard that Goodman Godfrey and his family were all safe in Genoa, having almost miraculously met together again when they landed in France; they

had found asylum with a leather merchant and Goodman Godfrey was at his old trade. Later, too, there
had come a message from Oliver, from the Low Countries, that had taken all of a year to find him. But
the most dearly sought news never came. It might be
that Edmund had left the King's service, that he was
seeking his fortune elsewhere, that he had become a
soldier—even that he was dead.

There was nothing for Simon to do but to wait
and to hope. . . .

Brother Josephus, the sacristan, had Simon by the
arm and was shaking him.

"Come now, wake up—wake up! The Archbishop
is asking for you to serve his early mass."

Simon struggled up through fathoms of deep sleep
and tried to understand what Brother Josephus was
saying.

"The Archbishop," the monk repeated. "Hurry.
Don't you hear me? He needs a server. Why a plain
brother won't suit him, the Saints alone know. Fetch
me young Simon Audemer, he says. And what do I
find? A sluggard rolled tight in his blanket!"

"Coming . . ." Simon mumbled. He never knew
how the monks managed with so little sleep, with
matins at midnight, lauds to follow, prime at seven
in winter and six in summer, then the first mass . . .

"You've a few minutes, only," insisted Brother Josephus. "In the chapel of St. Stephen. Come along
now—let me see you on your feet."

Simon pushed feebly at the blanket and staggered

to the floor. He stood shivering on the cold bare floor, while the scholars in the other beds lay snug. He started dragging on his clothes. It was very dark, and he fumbled his way toward the little anteroom, where there was a lamp burning, and where a pitcher of water stood with a good layer of ice in its neck. The cold made Simon gasp, but it woke him at last. He tidied himself up, had the usual difficulty over fastening his belt, pulled on his felt slippers, and then went fast down the stone steps, along the cloister and so to the church. He rushed to make his preparations, and by the time Archbishop Thomas came quietly along the cloister in his turn, Simon was ready to help him vest and to go with him to the chapel.

In the great church the various lamps and tapers, and the two or three cressets stuck into iron sconces on the pillars, made pools of warm light that the darkness quickly blotted up. There were already three or four masses in progress at various side chapels, and the Abbot himself at the high altar had reached the Gloria; he had a congregation of lay brothers and a handful of villagers who made a habit of attending on their way to work. The small murmur of the various celebrants and their acolytes, sometimes chiming, sometimes out of key, filled the body of the church with a sensation of busy, purposeful supplication. Hurry had warmed Simon's body; now his spirit was warmed, too. Perhaps for the first time, though he had been at Pontigny long enough to feel himself a part of the place, he wondered if this might be his life—this hard subduing of the body to the labor of unceasing prayer for those in the world and out of it. As he knelt on the altar steps and made his first responses, Simon was fired with magnificent intentions—but he was not very sure that he would ever have the strength to carry them out. He watched how the Archbishop seemed to submerge himself in the sacrifice, as though his body served merely to obey a few set rules of movement and speech, while his spirit was translated into some rarer communication. It seemed, Simon might almost have said, as though this was a man who spoke *with* God, rather than to Him.

Simon had often acted as Archbishop Thomas's server, but there was about this morning some special feeling which he could not explain to himself. Perhaps, he thought, Herbert of Bosham had put forward his suggestion of going as an envoy to the King, and the Archbishop was praying with particular earnestness for guidance. Yet this could hardly account for the fact that as the mass proceeded the celebrant grew increasingly pale and seemed almost to tremble. Indeed, as he held the chalice at the ablutions, his hands shook, and this affected Simon. He had always to be careful, and he had learned a way of clasping the small flasks of wine and water against his chest to steady them. This morning he fumbled badly and spilled some wine. He looked up in quick apology and concern, biting his lips. But he saw at once that the Archbishop had not even noticed.

As the mass proceeded to its end, Simon found that he was trembling himself, and when it came to carrying the missal across for the last gospel, he realized he was keeping the Archbishop waiting, though the Archbishop himself seemed unaware of this.

When the mass was at last ended, the Archbishop prostrated himself on the altar steps and lay so quietly there that Simon wondered if he had fainted.

The church was now intensely still. Archbishop Thomas had been the last to commence his mass. One by one the others had finished and gone away. The high altar and all side altars were empty. It was the pause before tierce, the next canonical office, and besides Thomas Becket and Simon there was no one present save two monks kneeling silently in the Lady Chapel.

Simon wondered whether he should move away, leaving the Archbishop to his devotions. Or whether, indeed, he should seek help, in case he were ill. But he knew that he should remain in order to leave the chapel with the priest, and so, uneasily, he stayed where he was.

The time spun on and still the Archbishop had not moved. Now Simon became aware of the small noises in the great building—a thin whistle of wind through an oaken door to his right; his own heart thumping in his ears; the faint, fussy twittering of a pair of starlings that had come inside the church in the winter weather and were now preparing to nest high in the roof . . . then the faintest pad of a slipper, its whisper on the stone floor, the flick of a gown as it swung against a pillar. He knew that someone had walked quietly toward the chapel and now stood unmoving in the shadows at the entry. He looked up, hopefully, expecting help, and saw that it was the Abbot who stood there.

At the same instant, Simon heard the Archbishop speak. His voice was low, not a whisper but a murmur.

"Who art thou, Lord?" he said.

He rose to his knees and seemed to listen. His face was uplifted and he was smiling. He was unaware of the Abbot and he had forgotten the boy kneeling on the lower step. He spoke again.

"May such bliss befall me indeed, O my Lord, that thy Church be glorified in my blood!"

Then, as though he had received an answer that filled him with unbearable joy, he covered his face with his hands and bowed his head till his brow touched the step before him.

At last, apparently unaware that there had been more than the usual pause, the Archbishop rose. When he turned to leave the altar, his face was that of a man who has received tidings more solemn, yet more joyful, than any ever hoped for.

They left the chapel as though nothing unusual had occurred, and it was only when Simon had helped the Archbishop to unvest that the Abbot joined them. Simon turned to the great chest where the folded vestments were laid, afraid that the Abbot might send him away. But both men seemed to have forgotten him. Their two voices were as unlike as air and water—the Abbot's dry and rebuking, the Archbishop's confident and proud.

"There was nothing that I could hear," the Abbot said.

"Thus was I answered: Verily my Church shall be glorified in thy blood; but when she is glorified through thee, thou shalt be honored by me."

"I heard none of this," insisted the Abbot.

"Then, father, speak nothing," the Archbishop said. He paused a moment; then he said, as though recalling words just heard that would never be forgotten: "O Thomas, Thomas—my Church shall be glorified in thy blood. . . . O Thomas, Thomas. . . ."

He moved away from the Abbot, who was frowning now. As though he had once again forgotten that he was not alone, he moved slowly away through the cloisters, his head bowed in thought or prayer, his arms folded in the wide sleeves of his gown: a tall, dark and lonely figure upon whose shoulders seemed to rest the hand of God.

V

To the King at Angers

THEY HAD BEEN hawking that morning, the last of April, and the sport had been good, so the King was in high spirits. He was a splendidly virile and energetic man, excellent company when he was

59

in humor. Because of this, his furies and frenzies, in which he seemed to be possessed by some devil, were all the more difficult to tolerate. After a spell at court, one became accustomed to the frenzies but dreaded them none the less. They were the occasion of too many personal disasters, of servants dismissed and courtiers degraded. And there was always the feeling that one day something irredeemable might result.

Returning from hawking, Edmund Audemer, with his friend Charles, who was page to Jordan Tarsun, went to the mews where the falcons were kept. Both he and Charles carried their masters' birds on their gauntleted left wrists. The falcons had to be seen safely into the care of the mews servants.

"Lys went well," Edmund said to the lad who had taken the hooded hawk from him. "The King praised her. But see to her jesses, if you please—there's a hint of wear in the skin."

The boy looked at the thongs that tethered the hawk and grimaced. They were of dogskin, soft and pliant.

"I was told to look to them three days ago. I'd have been in sore trouble if they'd snapped through! Thank you for showing me, Master Edmund."

The three boys stood together in the hawk house for a while, discussing the morning's sport; then Edmund and Charles left to pursue their various duties. Edmund was one of a host of pages in the King's personal service. Charles, one of two or three in a baron's household, was less concerned with immediate court routine.

Edmund had settled easily to this life. It was an extension of what he had known in his grandfather's castle, only grander and richer. He was the King's sworn vassal and must serve him according to his vow of allegiance, but he found no difficulty in that. There were only the occasional moments of doubt to trouble him—the moments of the King's rage, when he might turn on whoever was near and vent his fury with the most deplorable spite. There was no one among them who did not sometimes tremble to realize that he might be the victim one day or another. At such times, Edmund remembered how his brother Simon had spoken of seeking a place with the exiled Archbishop of Canterbury, and he wondered if he had ever reached that goal—and if so, which of the two brothers had the better lot. At night and morning he prayed for Simon, that he might be alive and well, and that even now they might meet again. . . .

When Edmund and Charles went indoors, they found a throng in the anteroom before the great hall. Men were standing about talking earnestly and eagerly, and there were half a dozen small groups arguing heatedly.

"What has happened?" Edmund asked Giles, one of the royal pages who was standing at the door.

"It's to do with the Archbishop of Canterbury," Giles replied. Then he stared at Edmund. "What's the matter? You've turned quite white. Are you ill?"

Edmund shook his head. "Not ill . . . The Archbishop, you say?"

"The King came in from hawking and found news that the Pope has made Archbishop Thomas his legate for all England. That started it all. There was a lot of noise, I can tell you! Roche told me the King threw his boots at the messenger's head!"

"Who was the messenger?"

"Oh, some poor priest tramped all the way in his sandals—Roche said he was swaying about and trembling like a reed in the river by the time the King had finished with him."

"Is that what they're talking about now?"

"No—this is about what happened next. The Archbishop has sent envoys to the King. Rumor has it they've already reached the town and gone to lodgings."

Now they were all arguing, Giles explained, as to whether the King would give these envoys an audience, or indeed whether he ought to do so. And whether or not the Archbishop had decided to be reasonable and make his peace with the King.

"What envoys are they?" Edmund cried. "Who has come? How many? Is there a train of them? Will the Archbishop himself come here, do you suppose?"

"You have as many questions as all the rest, Edmund! I know no more than I've told you—and that's all anybody knows. What is Archbishop Thomas to you?"

"I am thinking of my brother. He was to go into the Archbishop's service. When the decrees about the Archbishop's kin were made, my brother was lodging with some such, and he vanished with the rest. I have never discovered even if he is still alive. But if I could speak with the envoys—well, it is possible I might learn something."

The rest of the day went by in conjecture and rumor. At dinner time, when the King sat down to table in the great hall, he gave no sign of being in any way concerned with weighty matters. He ate hugely, his appetite sharpened by the morning's sport. Giles and Edmund were both in attendance at table. When the meal was ended, Giles carried the silver ewer for the King to wash his hands, a second page carried the pitcher, and Edmund handed the linen napkin. Occasionally the King would notice who was performing these rites, and today he looked up as Edmund handed the napkin. He spoke about the hawking.

"You have a way with a falcon, young Edmund Audemer. It was a gift your father had, too, they tell me."

"Yes, my lord," replied Edmund. "Hawking was the dearest sport to him."

The King handed back the crumpled napkin and Edmund bowed and moved away. He was pleased that the King had noticed him with the hawks and proud that his father should be remembered for his skill in falconry. It seemed to him that this might be a memorable day. It was as though, with the King's words and the news of the Archbishop's envoys his family was given back to him—often enough in the past year and a half it had seemed to Edmund that he had never had anyone of his own in the world.

By nightfall it was confirmed that the envoys were indeed in the town. Later, everyone knew that the King would receive them the next day, the first of May, which was Low Sunday.

The King kept the Archbishop's men hanging about in the antechamber for several hours. First he announced that he would see them immediately after early mass, then that he would break his fast before admitting them. Then it was learned that the encounter had been postponed until after high mass at midmorning. In the final event it was late in the afternoon when he called them before him at last.

The King had seen to it that the entire court was present. The hall hummed with the anticipation of everyone there. There were plenty who hoped to hear the Archbishop humbled through the King's treatment of his envoys. But others, for unity's sake, for the peace of England and the good of the Church, longed for a reconciliation.

"Who are the envoys?" Charles asked Edmund, under his breath. They were standing close by Charles's master, Jordan Tarsun, a blunt man given to speaking his mind, whether in the King's presence or out of it.

"John of Salisbury is one," replied Edmund. "And Herbert of Bosham, they say. I never saw either in my life before. They chose exile with the Archbishop, so Giles says."

The King at this moment turned to Reginald Fitz-Urse, one of his knights who was standing in close attendance.

"You may tell them to send in John of Salisbury," he said irritably. "The business has to be done."

The buzz of talk died away, and they all turned to watch FitzUrse as he crossed the floor and went himself into the anteroom. The King remained in conversation with those about him. When FitzUrse returned with John of Salisbury, that conversation continued, as the King seemed unaware that any newcomer had entered the hall—indeed it was as though he had instantly forgotten that the summons had been given.

Then John bowed his knee and saluted the King, and everyone was suddenly silent. John of Salisbury had a great, withdrawn dignity, and the silence was slightly shamefaced.

"Ah!" said the King, then, looking up with an air of having just recalled the business in hand. "Master John. It is a long day since you made obeisance to your King."

"It is my King who commands my exile," replied John, firmly but quietly.

"What is your business here?" King Henry asked, snapping his fingers impatiently. He was not prepared to bicker with insolent clerics.

"My lord King, I ask that I may be permitted to return to England in peace," said John of Salisbury.

This caused a murmur through the whole court, for they had expected the envoy to speak at once of his master, the Archbishop.

"I have never knowingly done anything to offend your Majesty," went on John. "You are my earthly ruler and I am ready, as I have always been, to serve you with devotion and fidelity."

"You have not always been ready to speak so humbly, however," replied the King. He turned to FitzUrse and laughed, as though he had made a point.

"I have always given due allegiance to my King," said John. "In all things saving only those that I owe first to God, through the Order whose habit I wear."

"Is it not true that you were born in my dominions? Are you not an Englishman? Why—your very name proclaims you, for they call you for your place of birth. This is so, is it not, John of Salisbury?"

"It is so, my lord."

"And since you have lived in my realm, you have lived under my protection—you have risen from the status of a humble clerk to that of one who might become a bishop. Since this is true—and you cannot deny it—it is for you to honor me, your King, in all things, and obey me—obey me, I say. Not sneak off to that enemy of mine, Thomas Becket."

"No enemy!" said John quickly and fervently. "Thomas Becket is many things—an Archbishop, a devout priest, the legate of the Pope for all England, your Majesty's loyal friend and subject. But no enemy—no enemy, my lord."

"We are not dealing with the Archbishop in any capacity save that of an enemy!" snapped the King. "We are not speaking of his loyalty, but of the loyalty of John of Salisbury. That should be a loyalty which would put his King before everything—a loyalty that should bind him to the King against all the rest of the world—including the Archbishop."

John smiled slightly and shook his head. They began to argue back and forth, the King containing his annoyance, the supplicant quietly refusing to concede any point. The King then proposed an oath of allegiance that would bind John of Salisbury to be faithful to him in life and limb, to defend the earthly honor of the King against all his enemies, to observe the King's law in all things, including those statutes drawn by his advisers which had some bearing on the conduct of church affairs.

"What statutes does your lordship mean?" asked John, warily.

"Swear to all this," said the King, ignoring the question, "and you are free to return in peace to England, and we ourselves will provide a safe conduct."

"But what statutes, my lord?" John insisted.

Close by the three young pages, who had been craning over the shoulders of their elders, Jordan Tarsun said under his breath to his neighbor: "He means those constitutions that were drawn at Clarendon. If we are to get back to that business, we are back at the beginning of the entire quarrel—we shall be here till midnight."

"Why," said King Henry, and he seemed to draw those about him into his confidence, as though directing their attention to his own cunning, "I mean those statutes or constitutions that were put to the Archbishop at Clarendon—that first he would not agree to, and then he was persuaded to agree to, and then, may he rue it! set aside contemptuously. For this men call him traitor—and for this, his own fault, he has gone voluntarily into exile—for I never decreed against him."

John of Salisbury was silent a moment. He was not only tired of exile but he knew that if he could get to England he could work for Archbishop Thomas's good. But the price of his desires was too high, and he sighed and shook his head.

"His Holiness the Pope has himself denounced certain of these statutes, sire. But I will swear to those articles among them which the Pope has admitted and approved, and which therefore his legate, the Archbishop, has also accepted."

The King leaned forward in his chair. His face had reddened and there was a familiar tremor in his voice that caused some quick looks and raised eyebrows among the court.

"Get back to him you have chosen for your master," he said. "Get back to him, John of Salisbury, since your allegiance is clearly not for your King. By God, I will not suffer one of you treacherous priests in my dominion for the very safety of my loyal subjects! Get you back to Archbishop Thomas and tell him that. Go now—go quickly, while I am still master of my rage."

John of Salisbury said no more. He bowed to the King and turned away. He faltered a little as he crossed the floor, as though his disappointment was almost too heavy for him. But he recovered himself quickly.

He lifted his head and straightened his shoulders and with great dignity he left the hall.

Edmund, watching him go, was filled with a sudden sensation of wretchedness. He did not enjoy seeing John defeated. He knew all the arguments that would be found in that place—that the King must be lord in his own realm, that those who questioned him could only be called treacherous. Why should Archbishop Thomas Becket set himself above the other bishops, who had accepted the King's intrusion into church affairs and were willing to abide by the new laws he had drawn up? Yet there was something more and Edmund, King's man though he was, knew it then as clearly as the Archbishop and John of Salisbury and all the others of their kind knew it. This was a matter outside politics. If the King had his way, he would be driving a wedge between the clergy in England and the Pope, leaving those within the Church no appeal but to the civil authority. Could that be justified? Edmund had never stopped to consider the matter before, but now, moved by John of Salisbury's great dignity, he frowned and wondered.

FitzUrse and the rest were crowding round the King and soothing him with flattery, telling him how strongly and well he had spoken to that crawling traitor, John of Salisbury—saying anything, in fact, to calm him and forestall the rage that had begun to boil in him, bloating his face and even his shaking hands, making his eyes bulge, as though fury strangled and choked him. Once such a fit really gripped him he was liable to roll on the floor and tear and bite at his clothing. Those about him had learned to act quickly if these repulsive displays were to be prevented.

When the King grew calmer, they asked him if he would see the second envoy.

"Who comes next to flout us?"

"It is Herbert of Bosham, sire."

The King gave a great guffaw at the name. "Send him in, by all means. Now you'll see a true picture of pride and arrogance! It will give me pleasure to hear Master Herbert plead!"

Then he restrained the courtier who would have gone to call Herbert of Bosham, sending instead a palace servant.

The interview with John of Salisbury had left others than young Edmund wondering and uneasy. They did not relish seeing another good man humbled, as humbled he most certainly would be now that the King's mood was so evil. There was a lack of dignity in this quarrel between powerful men that began to be distasteful to more thoughtful persons. They longed for peace between the King and the Archbishop, though they could not have said certainly from which side they expected the necessary concessions.

Then Herbert of Bosham entered. Unlike John, who had come alone to the King's feet with the modest dignity and aloofness of a man whose conscience is easy, Master Herbert strode in with a boy in attendance as though he were a man of substance and even power. The *picture of pride* which the King had anticipated had duly appeared, and a murmur of appreciation stirred the court. Men leaned forward to see the better, some standing up and peering over the heads of their fellows.

Herbert of Bosham wore a handsome green gown of Auxerre cloth. His cloak hung tossed from his shoulders and touched his heels. His ornaments were rich and fitting and, as he entered, he plucked from his head a fur-trimmed cap and handed it to his attendant.

From his place at the back of the hall, Edmund peered and craned his neck to get a better view. Then quite suddenly a man two rows ahead moved aside and there was a clear line through the throng to the figures standing before the King. A feeling of something very like nausea took Edmund. The boy attending Herbert of Bosham—could he be Simon? Could he indeed be the brother who had been six inches shorter when Edmund saw him last? Was he mad to suppose that this sober young clerk in sandals and cowled gown, his hair cut short as a monk's and lacking only the tonsure, was Simon Audemer, his twin?

"Let me see!" Edmund elbowed Charles furiously. Charles was shoved against Jordan Tarsun, who turned angrily and bade him mind his manners. Charles stood on Edmund's toe and Edmund was not even concerned to yelp. "I must see!" he muttered. "I must *see!* Charles—you are taller. Tell me quickly—can you see the left hand of the boy with Master Herbert?"

"That I cannot, for he carries it in his sleeve . . ."

At that moment, Jordan Tarsun leaned forward. Edmund had a sudden clear view. At the same instant, the other boy turned his head as though he had been summoned. He looked straight and unfaltering at Edmund. A very faint smile moved on his lips before he turned sternly back to attend his master.

"He is safe!" Edmund murmered. "He is safe and well! Oh I thank God for it. . . ."

The King was confronting Herbert of Bosham with all the questions he had put to John of Salisbury. But when King Henry spoke of Archbishop Thomas's treason, Herbert replied with none of John's meekness.

"The Archbishop is loyal above all men. Did he not see that his King was straying from a righteous path—and did he not give warning?" Before the King could find breath to answer this outrageous statement, Herbert had rushed on. "As for these statutes that were drawn at Clarendon—it was an evil thing, my lord King, to put them into writing. Thereby hung their downfall. In other kingdoms there are ill usages against the Church. But they are not written down. Therefore all honest men know there is good hope that they will soon fall into disuse."

"This is abominable!" shouted the King. "Is this son of a priest to disturb my kingdom and break my peace with his insolence?"

"It is not I who disturbs the King's peace," replied Herbert. His shoulders seemed straighter than ever and he did not scruple to fling back the insult that had been hurled at him. "Nor, my lord, am I the son of a priest. I was born long before my father took orders. He is not by right a king's son," he added, coldly and clearly, "whose father was not King when he was born."

At this, something near clamor broke out, for the insult could not have been more direct. Jordan Tarsun was heard to murmur: "Whoever's son this Herbert is, I would give half my land if he were mine. He is as brave as a lion."

The King's face flamed and swelled with his rage. He thumped with his fist and stamped his foot.

"Go!" he bellowed. "You are not fit for this presence! Get back to that which suits you better!"

Herbert of Bosham bowed formally. He took his cap from Simon, smiling at him slightly as he did so. Then he turned and strode from the hall with the boy at his heels.

As they vanished into the anteroom, tumult filled up the great hall they had left. Edmund began pushing and shoving his way through the excited press, caring little what exalted ribs he prodded, what dignified toes he trampled on. Nothing was of the least importance save that he should reach his brother before Master Herbert called for the horses and the whole embassy clattered away in fury.

An hour later, John of Salisbury was beginning to complain bitterly. The small train of servants and horses still waited for the word to depart. They were impatient of the delay and muttered together, as John of Salisbury was muttering to himself. The treatment they had received at the King's hands demanded a swift and dignified departure. Yet still they dallied.

"A moment more," said Herbert of Bosham, "and we will be well on our way." He glanced at John, who was standing somberly by his horse's head. "Mount and ride on, brother. We shall overtake you in an hour."

"This is absurd," said John of Salisbury, irritably. "The Archbishop will be expecting our return most anxiously. Yet we kick our heels here while we wait for the most insignificant of our train. You are too lenient."

Master Herbert smiled. "You are upset because we have been disappointed today."

"Insulted—bitterly insulted!"

"Disappointed, too. But these lads are scarcely more than children. Leave them a little longer."

Edmund had taken Simon into the little guard room by the gate, where the pikemen sheltered. The time was so short there was scarcely anything they could say. Yet they looked at each other with such delight and happiness that words were not so very necessary. They were twin, after all, and they had never needed to explain things to one another very much. In the delight of meeting after so long, they hardly realized that the parting already upon them might be even longer than the first. Nothing that had happened that day could give them much hope for the future.

"It is a mighty strange thing," said Edmund, "that you and I must depend for everything on the affairs of such great men. Who would have supposed that if we ever separated—it would be on account of kings and archbishops!"

"Let them be butchers and tailors and we'd be no better off," Simon replied. "We should still have our way to make." He sighed and then smiled. "But it is something, brother, that we are both alive!"

"It is everything. The times will mend and we shall be together."

Edmund spoke with great confidence. He seemed to Simon to be very grown up and experienced in the world. He was still the taller of the two. And since he lived in the palace of the King, he fared richly. He was twice as broad as Simon, who existed in the rigid frugality of a monastery.

Herbert of Bosham came to the door.

"We must leave now, Simon. Say farewell to your brother. Who knows, it may not be so long before you meet again. For all the King's rage, the Pope will not suffer his legate to be scorned. Say good-by cheerfully, then."

The brothers embraced. Now that the moment of parting had come, and so swiftly, it was hard to accept. Simon followed Master Herbert out to the waiting horses. Edmund gave him a leg up into the saddle.

"That's a scrawny beast you've got there," he said, grimacing. "Do you remember the horses in our grandfather's stable, and the little fierce Welsh ponies?"

Simon nodded. He remembered altogether too much of those days when, whatever else had happened, he could be sure that his brother would always be at his side.

The head of the train was moving off.

"Good-by!" Simon called in a croaking voice that shamed him. To make up for it, he wheeled his poor mount stylishly and was away. At least he would show Edmund that he had not forgotten how to ride, handicapped though he might be. He looked back once, and saw Edmund still standing there, a blurred figure with one arm uplifted in farewell.

VI

The Plain Near Montmirail, 1169

IT WAS THE FEAST of the Epiphany and the weather
was clear, cold and dry. The plain beyond Montmirail, where the French King Louis was just then in

residence, was dotted with small groups of horsemen. One might have supposed that forces were deploying for a battle. But the day's intention was a peaceful one, the atmosphere full of expectation. For a meeting of the Archbishop of Canterbury with the King of England had been brought about by the good offices of King Louis of France.

Ever since the meeting had been talked of, there had been no other topic for the small fry like Simon. The Archbishop had left Pontigny now and was at the monastery of St. Colombe. Simon had been glad when Eustace, the scholar who was his closest friend, had been attached to the household of the Archbishop and gone along with the rest.

"Now all will be well," these boys had assured one another. "With the help of King Louis, the King and the Archbishop will be friends again."

There had been many false attempts in the past three years to reconcile the two men. Scores of letters had been written by diligent scribes, with difficulty keeping up to the dictation of frenzied masters. Messengers by the dozen had scurried about Europe in the delivery of these letters, passing from England to France, from France to Italy, from the French King to the Pope, from the Pope to King Henry—and so on and on in seemingly endless permutation. There had been conferences, there had been quick, dangerous quarrels among clergy and laymen—threats of excommunication and appeals for aid that amounted to threats. . . . Now at last a meeting that seemed to offer hope of settlement had been brought about. Everyone was anxious; optimistic or not, according to temperament, but in every case tense and nervous.

The Archbishop had already arrived and was sitting his horse as he always did—with a splendid uprightness left over from the days when his horsemanship was his pride. Around him was a jostle of friends and advisers. There was hardly one who was not urging him to be moderate—to be reasonable—to yield a little, just a little of what he had refused to yield since he came out of England five years ago.

"It needs only a word to set all differences at rest. The King longs for reconciliation. Think, my lord. Think deeply."

"Since the King of France, who is your lordship's friend, is to mediate between you, surely all things are easier than ever before?"

"The two Kings of England and France have made their peace—they have signed a treaty to end all strife between them. Shall the Archbishop of Canterbury lag behind in generosity?"

And beneath it all came the cry most likely to move him—a cry weary and in fact unspoken, the exiles' cry for home: "Ah my lord, my lord—take us back to England where we belong!"

There was hardly need of words between them. They knew he longed to appease and content them, that he longed as much as they to return home. From John of Salisbury to young Simon Audemer, they watched him more intently than ever they had watched him before. His expression was stern, too familiarly so for their comfort. He had looked thus all the way from St. Colombe—where they had been ever since the King of England had frightened the Abbot of Pontigny into suggesting that his distinguished guest might move on. And all the way he had hardly spoken.

Simon, on a scruffy, restless bay pony, looked tensely from face to face. There they all were to advise and urge and conciliate—John of Salisbury, William Fitzstephen, Robert of Merton, Llewellyn the Cross-bearer, Herbert of Bosham—all waiting under the bland pale sunlight of the January day for some sign that their master would relent the fraction that was necessary for all their hopes.

At last the Archbishop said in a low, firm voice: "I will submit in all things—saving God's honor."

Some among them groaned. His old friend William, Archbishop of Sens, who had come to support him at the conference, cried out in anguish, "My lord, this will offend the King all the more! What do you impute to him—that he will not save God's honor? There is little to choose between this and 'saving the rights of my Order,' which set about the whole quarrel."

The Archbishop was silent. Time was running out. On the far side of the field there was movement among the King's men gathered there, a coming and a going, a mustering of banners. Soon the two Kings, with cries from the trumpeters to announce them, and riding horses splendidly caparisoned, would ride into view and take up their position. Soon would come an advancing herald with a summons for the Archbishop. Upon the approaching moment there depended far more than the comfort of a few exiles—there depended still the whole question of the Church in England, its freedom from interference by the sovereign, its freedom to communicate as it must with its true head, the Pope.

The crowd round the Archbishop had been increased by the arrival of many bishops and clergy of King Louis's train, come to add their words of encouragement and persuasion. Gradually, what had begun as an orderly conclave of solemn men became a clamor of insistent tongues.

Herbert of Bosham moved on the outskirts of the throng, listening warily to what was passing, and Simon nudged his pony up behind, obediently in attendance. Master Herbert had brought the boy with him partly out of kindness, since, if the day went well he would certainly see his brother. But there were practical reasons, too, for Simon's presence.

"Come with me and keep your wits about you," Herbert of Bosham had said. "I am much mistaken if we shall not have need of witnesses to what may pass. One way or the other, this is a day that will be remembered." And he put his hand on Simon's shoulder. "You will be here to remember and to record it long after we others have gone to our graves."

Simon had had at that moment a most extraordinary sensation. He felt he was being handed a trust that he must honor, and yet he could not see how this

was to be done. To remember—and to record . . .
Master Herbert's words had rung in his ears ever
since. . . .

Now there rang out a trumpet call. Silence fell
abruptly over the disputing group about the Archbishop. Sudden excitement ran like a wind across
the plain as a herald was seen advancing. Behind
him, breasting a slight rise in the ground, came the
two Kings, riding side by side, with a train of attendants. Then the French King reined in his black horse
and motioned the English King a little aside. They
drew in together under a cluster of trees and waited.
The breath from the horses' nostrils made a cloud
on the air before them, as the splendid creatures nodded and tossed their heads till their harness jingled,
and pawed at the hard wintry ground under their
hoofs. Pulling into a rough semicircle, discreetly withdrawn to ten paces or so, the nobles and attendants
gathered about the two Kings.

The herald moved on, approaching the Archbishop.
Instead of proudly awaiting the summons to the royal
presence, the Archbishop shook his bridle and urged
his horse on. The rest copied him, and the whole
crowd surged forward.

Herbert of Bosham moved sharply and impulsively.
He began pushing through the throng of advisers until he reached the Archbishop's elbow.

"Take care, my lord," he said urgently, "and walk
warily. If you suppress these words *saving God's honor*,
your sorrow will be renewed."

Archbishop Thomas turned and smiled at his old friend. There was no time for him to reply. But he nodded slightly. Then he and his attendants were moving forward again. The rest of them followed at a suitable distance, placed as well as they could manage, in support as they had always been and barely admitting that many of them today demanded more of him than had ever been demanded. William of Sens overtook the Archbishop and moved into position at his side; it had been decided that for dignity's sake the two archbishops should make an obeisance to the King together.

Simon pushed up behind Herbert of Bosham, peering over his shoulder at the opposite ranks attendant on the Kings. He was torn between the drama he was there to witness and the longing to find Edmund among the rest. Though the brothers had had word of one another during the past three years, they had met only twice, and that hurriedly. In the ranks of unfamiliar faces Simon could find no focus. All were intent upon what was to take place. Some smiled; some frowned; some sneered; some looked severe. It was impossible to pick out Edmund. There was only the color of cloak and tunic, the flash of jeweled pins and chains, the gleam of costly rings; the strange variety of complexion, from blond to swarthy; the way one face would suddenly stand out among the rest by the certain statement in eye or mouth or brow that here was a man to be reckoned with. . . .

A murmur from those about him forced Simon's

attention back to the principals in this scene. Without waiting for William of Sens, the Archbishop had thrown himself from his horse and knelt like any vassal before the King. And the King himself, as though moved immeasurably by this gesture, remembering old times and eager for reconciliation, was out of his own saddle in a second and raising his old friend up eagerly.

Then he held the Archbishop's stirrup while he remounted, turning to his own horse only when Thomas Becket was settled into the saddle.

Splendid omens! Everyone was smiling.

"Have mercy on me, O my lord King," cried the Archbishop. "And on that Church of which by the Pope's election and your favor I am the unworthy head!"

The King checked, minutely but instantly, and a faint sigh was heard among those near at hand.

"Of those troubles which have stood between us," the Archbishop went on, "how many are to be laid at my door?" And he began to speak in his fine ringing voice of the miseries of the past few years, blaming himself for the disorder and wretchedness that had come between him and his King, and breathing no word now of condemnation.

The King sat rigidly and listened. The first impulsive generosity and affection had ebbed from his expression; his slightly lowered head showed wariness and suspicion. Unlike the King of France, whose whole countenance beamed with his pleasure in bringing about an encounter which he was convinced could only end well for all of them, King Henry bristled with doubts.

"Therefore, my lord King," concluded Thomas Becket, "on this whole subject that lies between us I throw myself on your mercy and on your pleasure—here, in the presence of his Majesty the King of France, and of the archbishops, princes and others who stand around. . . . Saving only the honor of God himself."

The King let out a great bellow of fury.

"Hear that, my lord!" he cried to King Louis. "Now believe me that this is an arrogant priest whose pride in himself must be heard to be understood! And this is the man I raised from obscurity and treated as my friend. The man to whom I gave the highest office—in the realm, then in the Church! And what has he done but abuse and betray me? If ever there was a traitor—that is he!"

All Simon's dreams of being reunited with his brother were dwindling away. He was filled with a sudden childish longing to stamp and cry, to hammer at the Archbishop whose obstinacy was ruining all their lives. . . . Then from far in the past he heard a faint echo of a voice he thought he had long forgotten, the voice of the King's steward at the Tower of London. *When great men quarrel we all must suffer. . . .*

"My lord King knows well the falsity of his words," said the Archbishop, steadily.

King Henry seemed to sweep him aside as he swung round once more to the King of France.

"See here, my lord," he shouted, "how vain and foolish a man this is. For he himself deserted his church, though none demanded he should do so. He ran away—like a coward, by night—though neither I nor anyone else drove him from the kingdom. And now," he cried, with a great roar of frustration, "he seeks to convince you that he suffers for justice's sake—that his cause is the cause of the Church. He has deceived many just and holy men—I know that well. Do not, my lord, let him deceive you!"

Then he went on to speak of the constitutions made at Clarendon, and how the Archbishop had refused to countenance them at the last, when he learned they must be irrevocably written down. Yet many of these constitutions or customs, the King claimed, had been in use for generations.

"This is all the substance of our quarrel," he insisted. "I ask for nothing more than that the Archbishop shall keep those customs which his five immediate predecessors all observed to mine. And some of these men were saints! God's eyes, my lord King, this is not much to ask."

Someone called out: "The King humbles himself enough!"

"Too much! Too much!" cried another.

At this the Archbishop was again utterly still and silent.

"Come, my lord Archbishop," said King Louis. "You have heard your King speak of your predecessors in the see of Canterbury. Those were great and holy men. Do you wish to be more than a saint?"

He smiled a little, as though to take the offense from his words. But it was plain enough that he was swayed by the vehemence of the King of England, and that for the first time he began to see Archbishop Thomas through the eyes of his adversary.

"Why do you doubt, my lord?" King Louis insisted. "Here is peace at hand."

"It is true," said Thomas Becket in a low voice, "that my predecessors were greater and better than I. We blame Peter for denying Christ, but we praise him for opposing Nero. . . . Shall I, therefore, to recover a man's favor, suppress God's honor?"

The King broke in, raging. "This phrase I will never accept—never! Am I to be accused of denying God's honor—of failing in my duty and devotion? Am I so much less a man of God than this—this leather merchant's son?"

"Give the King due honor!" someone shouted. "Submit yourself to his will and pleasure. Now or never is the time for reconciliation."

The Archbishop's advisers, forgetting the courtesies due to the two monarchs, now surrounded Thomas Becket, urging him to relent, to give in for the sake of peace. But he would only shake his head, turning from one to another as though hoping for understanding and sympathy.

"And do remember, my good lord," he said to the King, "that in the oath of fealty itself, by which your vassals give their allegiance and their lives in service to the throne, there is still this saving clause that places God's honor above all—which then your Majesty accepts in good faith!"

"Enough!" cried the King, wheeling his horse. "He condemns himself. There is no hope for anyone here—leave him—leave him. . . ."

With this he dug spurs into his horse's sides and rode off, shouting and cursing against impudent, arrogant men.

For a moment or two King Louis remained. He seemed defeated and distressed. Now for the first time he did not go to the Archbishop to comfort or reassure him. He called shortly to his nobles and himself followed the English King.

The moment the two Kings were gone, fury and confusion broke out among the courtiers, among the French and the English, the clerics and the laymen. And not least of those who shouted and argued in furious disappointment were friends of the Archbishop—not the closest, maybe, but many who had seemed to love him. They saw their hopes of home fading, and their misery made them cruel.

"Why," they cried, "must we be better than our fathers?"

Even the French nobles had set store by the reconciliation.

"All is now lost," some cried. "And through the arrogance of the Archbishop."

"He is rejected by England," said another. "Let him find no countenance or support in France."

The Archbishop had remained still and upright as

ever until this. But now he turned and with his head a little bowed he began to move away. With all the rest, Simon followed. He was now so stirred with wretchedness by the plight of Thomas Becket that he hardly cared for his own disappointment at not seeing Edmund after all.

In silence they rode away from the now deserted plain to the palace of Montmirail where the Archbishop was lodged by the hospitality of the King of France. For how long, now, perhaps he wondered. Herbert of Bosham urged his horse up close behind his friend and master, with Simon following in dutiful attendance. As they rode away, there was no sound but the jingling of harness and the ring of hoofs on the hard frosty ground.

Then ahead, somewhere in the file, a horse stumbled and the rider plucked hard at the bridle.

"Come up!" he said, his voice clear and mocking on the quiet evening. "Come up—saving the honor of God—and of the Church—and of my Order."

Everyone looked shocked and glanced sideways at the Archbishop, who gave no sign of having heard. But he called out to them all to hurry, and spurred his horse forward, and all rode hard until they had reached the summit of a hill; there they checked to breathe the horses.

"My dear companions, my faithful brethren," said Thomas Becket to those nearby, "you who have suffered everything with me—why do you so speak and think against me?"

"It is our sadness, no more," said Master Herbert, quickly.

"Our return is but a little thing," said Thomas Becket. "The liberty of the Church, of which the King says nothing, is all that matters. At length I will accept the best peace I can. But not yet. This is poor bargaining."

"Him will I honor who honoreth me," quoted Herbert of Bosham softly, for the Archbishop alone.

It was too dark to see if the Archbishop smiled and looked comforted.

The plight of this small fellowship of exiles seemed likely to be worse than ever before. In the past it had always been possible to rely on King Louis. But there seemed little hope of his continuing favor. Coldly, Simon realized that he was further from Edmund than he had ever been. What traffic could there be now between the Archbishop's household and the King's court?

Next morning, having had no word at all from their host, the King of France, they set out on the return journey to St. Colombe. As they rode through the towns and villages, the people paused to watch them go, and asked whose train this was.

"There goes the Archbishop of Canterbury!" cried one. "He would not deny God or neglect His honor for the sake of two mighty monarchs."

Excitement seized the people. They ran beside his horse, shouting praises of his steadfastness. Word of the conference at Montmirail had moved ahead of them in the magical fashion of country news, and all the rest of the way there was this gathering of peasants and artisans to cheer them home.

It seemed strange to Simon to be back once more at St. Colombe. He had expected so much of the meeting and now he did not know how to order his thoughts. Like all of the rest, he spent much time wondering how long they would be allowed to remain in the monastery, and where, without the King's support, they would find their next lodging. When they were in the cloisters in the afternoons, in the time of leisure, this was what they spoke of most.

"I will go away," the Archbishop said, when he was sitting among them. "I am the only one among you whom King Henry wishes to injure. Therefore, do not be afraid."

"It is for you that we take thought, father," said William Fitzstephen. "We do not see where you can find refuge."

"Your friends have deserted you," lamented Llewellyn. "Though you are so high in dignity, they have abandoned you."

"Do not care for me," he replied. "I commend my cause to God, who is very well able to protect me."

"But where will you go?" they insisted.

"Perhaps to Burgundy, where they say men are more liberal. Perhaps I will take one companion and go among those people on foot. They will assuredly have compassion on me." He looked thoughtfully round his companions as he spoke, as though he wondered which of them he might choose.

Someone was hurrying along the cloister from the great gateway, It was the porter, with his keys dangling and clashing together as he came almost running to the Archbishop.

"My lord, you are summoned to King Louis," he said. "You must go to him at once, the messengers say."

"It is as we feared," Llewellyn murmured. "He means to turn us from his kingdom."

The Archbishop laughed. "Are you a prophet, or the son of prophets? Do not forbode ill, Llewellyn."

He rose vigorously, calling to Herbert of Bosham and William Fitzstephen, and his steward Osbert to attend him. Simon leaped hopefully in Master Herbert's shadow, but was obliged to drop back when he received only a headshake.

"You are growing vain, Simon Audemer," said Eustace, who had been a scholar at Pontigny and was now attached to the household. "Do you expect to be a counselor of archbishops?"

Simon did not reply. He sat uneasily wondering what was to happen next. It was difficult for all of them to wait in patience for whatever news was to come.

It was Osbert the steward who finally brought the answer to all their conjecture.

"The Archbishop tells me to reassure you all. King Louis has thrown himself at our master's feet and begged forgiveness for having doubted him."

"He has changed his mind. . . ."

"The English King has changed it for him," replied

the steward. "He has broken the new treaty and is marching against Poitou. Deceived on one count, King Louis realizes he has been deceived on others." Osbert gave a sudden dry chuckle. "I think it must be the first time that any one of us here has had cause to give thanks to King Henry of England!"

VII

A Ship for England, 1170

IT WAS POOR weather for traveling, and it seemed a very long way from Sens to the coast. Simon was saddlesore by the end of the first day. What had become so familiar to him in the past years was now

left far behind. Ahead lay England and whatever perils or joys that might offer. They were going home at
last. But as they set out muffled against the November
weather, a train of a hundred or more, well mounted,
and escorted by Count Philip of Flanders, there was
plenty of cause for anxiety.

"I keep thinking of the Archbishop's words to the
Bishop of Paris," Simon said to his riding companion. "Did you hear?"

"I was not there as you were," replied the young
clerk, Gilbert. "But I know well enough and I urge
you not to repeat the words."

The Archbishop had said: *I go to England to die.*

The final reconciliation between King and Archbishop had come suddenly. It was brought about by a
matter that might seem to have little connection with
the quarrel. Occupied as he was with affairs in his
French dominions, King Henry had long been concerned at leaving England to be governed by states-
men. He needed his eldest son, Prince Henry, as his
proxy. The boy must be crowned King of England.
The coronation of the monarch was the right of the
Archbishop of Canterbury.

"There *is* no Archbishop of Canterbury," the King
had declared.

Ignoring the Pope's warning that none but Canterbury could officiate, the King made his own arrangements. Prince Henry was crowned by the Archbishop of York on June 14, 1170. To distinguish him
from his father, he was known as the Young King.

It was in fact this very defiance that led to the

reconciliation of King and Archbishop. The King had been obliged, in some alarm, to placate the furious Pope. He gave in. The Archbishop should be restored to Canterbury, his disciplinary rulings were to be upheld, his authority was to be recognized and all should now be as he wished.

It might have seemed that all was well at last, but for one thing.

"Why, *why* did the King not give the kiss of peace?"

There was not a man among those traveling home with Archbishop Thomas who did not ask himself this question a dozen times and more each day. The kiss of peace was the salute demanded by convention when such quarrels as this one were concluded. Without it, the treaty between the two great men seemed flimsy indeed. And worse than that, it had been whispered that the King meant to have the Archbishop killed, and that by refusing the kiss he avoided the extra burden to his conscience.

Besides, there had been a number of needless insults, petty in themselves but disturbing as they accumulated. None of this, however, had deflected the Archbishop from his purpose of returning to England. At the start of the journey he had indeed seemed morose and unapproachable, as though burdened intolerably by his own thoughts. Then he had roused up and become more his usual self. A feeling of relief had spread through the column. They tried to set aside their doubts and told themselves instead that in ordering the Archbishop home the King had conceded much. The Pope, too, had not only urged

the return, but had approved and confirmed Archbishop Thomas in his determination to put down
his proved enemies. The unlawful and defiant crown-
ing of the Young King would be punished by sentences of excommunication. Supported, then, by both
King and Pope, why should the return of the Archbishop be anything but a joyful occasion?

"The last time I crossed the sea," Simon told Gilbert, "I was only eleven years old. I was parted from
all I knew. . . . I feel almost as much a stranger now
I am returning to my own country."

"Canterbury is home," said Gilbert. "She is our
mother and will care for us. You have nothing to
fear."

"It is not only myself I fear for."

"What befalls our master," was the reply, "can befall nothing more substantial than his body. His spirit
is sure."

Simon did not reply. He looked at Gilbert sideways and tried not to feel irritated with him. Gilbert
would one day be an ordained priest but Simon had
realized by now that he himself had after all no vocation. He was no longer a child but a young man
of seventeen whose eyes were opening on the world.
Sometimes he thought he would ask the aid of Herbert of Bosham to get to Paris or Florence to study
law. But the time somehow was not ripe. At this moment every servant and friend of Archbishop Thomas must feel bound to remain at his side. In his
most secret thoughts, Simon felt himself, perhaps
presumptuously, to be as dedicated as any of the many

young clerks employed in the Archbishop's household. He had never forgotten Herbert of Bosham's words on the day the Archbishop met the two Kings on the plain near Montmirail. He had spoken of needing witnesses—he had seemed to select Simon for a particular task without explaining just what that task should be. And he had said, only a few days later, when Simon was writing to his dictation: "What words would you choose, boy? Let me see what you make of the letter." Then Simon wrote a whole letter on his own account. He had been pleased and flattered when it went to its destination with no erasures.

Since then he had taken to writing down accounts of this and that, using scraps of spoiled paper and hoarding them in the satchel where he kept his pens and his inkhorn.

Simon thought about this matter a great deal. But as he rode on his way to the coast with Gilbert rather too piously riding beside him, he thought more of that other time he had crossed the channel. Where was Brother Oswin now? With a soft, warm smile he remembered the goodness of Dame Joan and her husband, the friendliness of their children. Hugh and Roger were a year or two older than he was—why, they might almost be married by now! He could recall them cheerfully, for he had received and dispatched greetings to them in Genoa more than once. Only last Christmas, Dame Joan had sent him, by a servant of her husband's traveling to England, a great round cake stuffed with plums and almonds and butter. Although it was a very unsuitable gift for a humble clerk attached to a monastery and living austerely, Simon and three of the scholars who were his particular friends had smuggled it away and eaten it in the herb garden after dark—to the astonishment and dismay of four stomachs accustomed to the plainest fare.

Simon grinned to himself as he remembered. One of the scholars had been Eustace, whose gown had never quite concealed the fact that he was a rich man's son accustomed to a softer way of life. He had startled them all a few months later by offering himself as a candidate for the monastic life. He wished to become a Benedictine, like the Archbishop. He was riding now behind Simon and Gilbert, and for him the journey was a joyous one, since at Canterbury he would begin his novitiate.

Gradually the miles to the coast unwound themselves. At Male, the Count of Flanders gave them hospitality, and the Archbishop was pressed to consecrate the newly built chapel there. Then they moved on again, and came to St. Omer.

"This is familiar country," Herbert of Bosham told Simon. "Here the Archbishop came in the first days of his exile. And here I joined him, with the money and servants that he needed. Then I heard all the tales of his landing—how he was helped and how he was recognized even in disguise. He stopped for a while at an inn, and the landlord's wife knew him instantly. Not by his great height, she said, nor by his long white hands, but by his gentleness with the children, and the way he gave them the best bits of meat from his plate."

Herbert's voice ran on over stories long familiar to Simon. But he knew the telling of the tales gave Master Herbert great pleasure. He was moved as always to consider the faithful service Herbert of Bosham had given the Archbishop, going with him into exile, sharing his sorrows, and now returning to face whatever the homecoming might hold.

Not that Herbert of Bosham was the only stalwart. There was John of Salisbury—who had gone ahead to England and would send them a ship—and others like William Fitzstephen and Alexander Llewellyn. As Master Herbert often said of Llewellyn, words were not his only virtues, for though he was prompt in his tongue he was prompter still in action, and he was as faithful as he was clever. Besides these, and Robert of Merton, there were others who had come at varying times and now rode homeward—Gunter of Winchester, Gilbert Glanville, Randulf de Sera, and many servants not in Orders, under the charge of Osbert the steward. For these the return must be at least an occasion of reunion with their families.

In the great Abbey of St. Bertin the whole company rested gratefully. Now the coast was very near, and the moment when they must embark appeared to some a moment of great apprehension. In spite of all the King had promised, in spite of the Pope, in spite of their own self-assurances, there was nothing to tell them of the temper of the people.

Next morning, the journey was resumed under the guidance of Peter, Abbot of Ardres, who was to escort them to the castle of the Count of Guisnes. Some time after noon, Abbot Peter checked his horse and pointed to the west.

"There, my lord Archbishop, stands the Abbey of Ardres. I pray you, though you may not enter under its roof today, let your blessing rest upon it."

Archbishop Thomas laid his right hand for a moment upon the Abbot's sleeve. Then he raised his hand in benediction toward the distant abbey.

Eustace nosed his lean horse up to Simon's side.

"It is almost as though his hand rested upon the abbey," he said.

Simon did not reply. He looked toward the tall figure in its muffling cloak, and he felt some of that aloof reverence he had known on the morning he served mass at St. Stephen's altar, and the Archbishop had seemed to be talking with his God. . . .

At that moment, Count Baldwin de Guisnes rode out at a gallop to greet Archbishop Thomas, throwing himself impulsively from his saddle, catching at the Archbishop's bridle and bowing his head against the sandaled foot in the stirrup. It was a curious encounter. Years ago, when Thomas Becket was still Chancellor of England, he had knighted the young Baldwin, according to the custom and law of chivalry. Now, he bent from his saddle to embrace his host, raising him with one hand and smiling with pleasure at meeting so old a friend.

The splendor of the Count and his followers, their magnificent horses and accoutrements, reminded Simon of his brother Edmund, who still lived in the richness and comfort of the King's court. Obeying an old habit, Simon glanced down at his left hand, the only circumstance that had led him into so different a way of life from Edmund's. He frowned. He knew that this hand, though its fingers appeared limp, yet somehow grasped an invisible key. It was the secret of his past and present, that much he knew. What he also knew, though in a confused fashion only, was that it held the greater secret of his unknown future.

When they reached the coast and came to the spot where they were to embark, there was no ship waiting. The weather had been poor, they were told, with an offshore wind. Now it was calm enough but the vessel they expected had not been sighted. They gazed on the quiet sea and knew that they must reconcile themselves to waiting.

The Archbishop grew troubled about the sentences of excommunication that were to be passed on the Bishops of London and Salisbury for their part in the coronation of the Young King; and the sentence of suspension of all his religious duties which would be imposed upon the Archbishop of York. He feared that some messenger from the King, setting off from another port, might reach England and warn the culprits of what was to come. Archbishop Thomas was convinced that if he was to maintain a position of strength he must strike hard and without mercy. Therefore, it was decided to send letters ahead to deliver the sentences in writing.

"Osbert is your man," Herbert of Bosham said. "He is tough and guileful and devoted. He will not be afraid to cross the water in a small boat—there are many fishermen who will undertake the journey if they are well paid."

Simon was given the task of making copies of the letters. The thunderous words of the sentences almost made him tremble as he wrote them. Then they were dispatched by Osbert, who set about getting to England in his own way.

And still the ship had not arrived to take the Archbishop and his following home.

They would walk along the shore in the sharp winter weather, watching the sea and the sea birds, and what traffic of a small sort moved about the harbor. And they would look at the sky and try to predict the weather, and pray for their ship, and for a continuing wind to carry them home. So small a strip of water separated them from the coast of England that their eager eyes seemed almost to see the white line of the cliffs.

On the morning after the dispatch of the messengers, they were joined on the shore by Milo, Dean of Boulogne.

"You come to speak of the arrangements for our journey!" the Archbishop said at once. No doubt from higher ground their ship had been sighted and the Dean brought word to them.

"That is not my business," replied the Dean. "I bring you a message from the Count of Boulogne. He bids you beware. He has news that the English coast is beset with enemies. They will either murder you or take you prisoner as soon as you land."

For a second the Archbishop was utterly still. This was the first open expression of what might lie in store, the first spoken warning to give force to his own forebodings.

"It is of no consequence to me," he said at last, in a low voice. "If I am to be torn limb from limb, I will go."

"My lord, consider—"

"It is now seven years since my church has been deprived of a pastor. It is my request, perhaps my last request, to my friends, that if I cannot return to Canterbury alive—they will carry me there dead."

At these words, a shudder was felt among those standing close at hand. No one dared to look at his neighbor, but stood with head bent, silent and full of fear. But the Archbishop immediately went on to speak of other things.

A day or two later they were all walking on the shore as usual when someone called out that a ship was coming in. They watched its approach eagerly. The younger men, Simon and Eustace and Gilbert among them, ran to the water's edge. The ship soon rode at anchor and a small boat came in to the beach. The ship was indeed from England, and though it was not the one they expected, there was news.

"At home there is nothing but talk of the excommunications," one sailor said. "The Archbishop's messengers met the bishops as they were setting out to join the King in France."

"Then the sentences have been served?" asked Eustace.

"Ay, they have, brother. And with much wailing and fury from their lordships."

"But the people," Simon said. "What do the people say about the Archbishop of Canterbury's return?"

"They rejoice! They long for their shepherd back among them. The people know the great goodness of their Archbishop. Ah, he has been sorely missed these years."

"Come and speak with him," Simon urged impulsively. "Tell him this. For we hear nothing but warnings of disaster."

But though the seamen insisted that the Archbishop was longingly awaited, the captain of the ship had a different tale to tell.

"What folly is this?" he cried, drawing Herbert of Bosham aside. "Are you mad? Do you not know that you are going to your death?"

"The sailors have said that the people rejoice—"

"It is not the people who will take the Archbishop, but the officers and barons of the King."

"Is it possible . . . ?" Herbert frowned and shook his head.

"The Young King's party, too, is exasperated against Lord Thomas. They say that even before he lands he has thrown everything into confusion. The clergy are scandalized because this is the season of Advent, when peace and tranquillity should be kept among us."

"I will tell the Archbishop what you say," said Master Herbert gloomily.

When Archbishop Thomas was told of this, he turned to those about him. He saw their grave and anxious faces. Although he had already said that he would return to England whatever threatened, he took pity on the rest and asked them for their counsel. They were gathered about him as though they would shelter and protect him from the world. What, then, would they have him do?

"If I were asked my advice," said Gunter of Winchester, "I should say we had better not go on just at present."

"This is coward's counsel!" cried another.

"We should remain quiet until this matter is a little blown over," insisted Gunter. "It will be still worse when the King comes to hear of the sentences passed on the bishops."

"I have the King's own word that I must deal sternly with the Church's enemies."

"He will not remember that," said Gunter.

"What do you say, Herbert?" Thomas Becket asked, turning to his old friend.

"My lord, it is difficult for me to hazard an opinion. It is a pity our learned John of Salisbury is not with us. He would know how best to advise."

"But what do *you* say, Herbert?"

"I say, my lord, that if we go back after having bidden farewell to all our friends out of England, and having got the Pope's license and blessing, it will be greatly to our disadvantage. We shall be dishonored."

Someone cried out angrily, "Would you condemn our master to death?"

"If I did so, it would be to martyrdom," said Herbert, steadily.

The Archbishop smiled at Herbert of Bosham.

"Truly," he said, "by God's help I will enter England—though I know for certain my death awaits me."

After that, he returned to his lodging and for a long while he spoke to no one.

On the first of December, very early in the morning, the wind blew strongly and their ship at last was waiting. Then began the great bustle of going aboard, of saying farewell to those who had ridden in escort and must now return the way they had come. But first these knelt on the shore. As he entered the small boat that would carry him out to the ship lying at anchor, the Archbishop stood for a moment to give them his blessing.

Then at last they were aboard. The anchor was weighed and the ship, her sail proudly filling, breasted out across the water. Fearing that Dover might indeed be filled with hostile forces, they set their course for Sandwich. This was very fitting, for it was from Sandwich that the Archbishop had set out upon his exile, all those weary years ago.

The mood of quiet strength that had settled over Thomas Becket remained with him. He stood in silence, staring across the sea to the southwest. As the weather was fair, it was not long before they sighted home. There was the sudden line of white upon the horizon, the sun sharp on the chalky coast.

"Look, my lord," cried Simon, who was standing near him. "There is England!"

At the cry, others hurried forward, craning their necks and narrowing their eyes for this first sight of home.

The Archbishop shook his head at their eagerness.

"Before we have been there forty days," he said, "I fear you may wish yourselves anywhere else in the world. . . ."

VIII

Homecoming

THE WIND remained fair. The sky bulged with immense clouds so white that they sharpened the winter blue. At last the voyagers drew near to the shore at Sandwich.

109

Immediately, the beach was filled with running figures hurrying to gather at the water's edge. Then the Archbishop ordered his cross to be set up, as a sign to the people that it was indeed he who approached. When the cross was seen, the excitement increased. Many of those who had gathered ran into the water as though they could not wait to greet their returning pastor. The sound of their voices came across the waves and seemed to swell about the ship in a great cry of welcome. And as the ship dropped anchor, as the Archbishop was rowed ashore, the cries became shouts that burst joyfully on the ears of those who were coming home.

"What of the threats now?" cried Herbert of Bosham. "This is a welcome indeed!" He was smiling broadly, he could hardly contain his pleasure. The roar of greeting seemed to sweep away all the warnings that had gone before. This, surely, was the answer to every question. "My lord, my lord!" cried Master Herbert. "These are your own people!"

Now the boat was about to touch bottom. Those who had rushed into the water surrounded the boat and pushed and pulled it to the beach.

"Father!" they cried. "Father!" And they took his robe in their hands and bent to kiss it—or his sleeves —or the long rough cloak he had put round him against the weather.

When he was ashore, the people crowded up to him, the women pushing their children forward to see him, or holding them up for his blessing. Excitement and a deep fervor ran over the whole throng, and they prayed and sang loudly. It was as though a great holiday had been proclaimed and here, at its very core, they could celebrate it with the keenest enthusiasm.

Now indeed Archbishop Thomas could afford to smile again. His face glowed with the happiness of this simple homecoming. He raised his hand to bless his people; he put his hands tenderly on the heads of the children; twice he took up in his arms one too small to stand, and held it while he signed the little creature's brow with his thumb.

Then, without warning, there was a shouting from behind the crowd and the sound of hoofs crunching on the beach. The people began to scatter and fall back, protesting and angry. Above their heads could be seen men in steel caps forcing a way through the mob, which had to part or be trampled by the horses.

"It is Ranulph de Broc!" someone cried.

The tone of the crowd now changed abruptly. The cries of welcome turned to angry, uneasy grumblings. Women ran together. Children began to cry.

As the crowd parted to let the mounted men through, the Archbishop's party, particularly the younger men, moved up protectively on all sides of him.

"They are armed!" Simon cried to Eustace. "They may wear tunics and cloaks, but you can see the hard steel beneath."

"We should have been warned and stayed in France. These are angry men, Simon!"

The name of de Broc had made Simon shudder. It reminded him of the nightmare journey to the coast of the so-called kin of the Archbishop, six whole years ago. De Broc must always remain in Simon's thoughts as the man who had separated him from his brother.

"Stay close," he muttered to Eustace. "If we have to fight, you have two good hands to my one."

Besides de Broc, there were the Sheriff of Kent, Gervase, and Reginald de Warenne, a kinsman of the King.

"You were expected at Dover, my lord Thomas," said Gervase, irritably. "As doubtless is known to you —since you sneak in this way."

"Before you are on English soil you cause trouble and dissension!" cried de Warenne. "By what authority do you proscribe and suspend and excommunicate? These are the King's bishops you treat so. His Majesty will be greatly offended."

"The King gave permission to punish those who injured my church," replied the Archbishop steadily. "Have not these bishops done so? And is the Pope's authority, in whose name I pronounce sentence, to be set at naught?"

"Absolve the bishops!" cried de Broc, breaking in on the others, thrusting his horse forward until he towered over the Archbishop, tall as he was.

"We will speak of this later," was the reply.

The three armed men moved together abruptly and spoke in low tones. Then Reginald de Warenne came forward again.

"If there are any foreigners with you—whether priests or clerks or monks or servants, I care not—let them swear an oath of allegiance to the King."

"This is the oath proposed for spies!" cried Gunter de Winton.

"And not imposed upon the clergy," said the Archbishop. "Therefore, it will be sworn by none here with me." He raised his head and looked imperiously at de Warenne. "My lord, you are to let us go on our way. We have nothing to say to one another."

De Broc laughed. "Not today, perhaps," he said. "But another day, my lord Archbishop Thomas Becket of Canterbury."

The crowd was now recovering from its cowed reception of the intruders. The muttering was no longer subdued, it broke out into angry, threatening cries. Those who had fallen back into a defensive huddle now moved forward once more. It was noticeable that the women and children had been pushed to the rear; the men and boys came forward steadily. Some carried stones taken up from the shore, others had sticks of driftwood gathered from among those lying along the tide mark.

"Give us the Archbishop!" someone cried. This was taken up and gradually rose into a great shout. "The Archbishop! The Archbishop for Canterbury! Clear the way!"

The three noblemen, with their posse of armed men, remained hesitant a second longer. Then Gervase wheeled his horse, and with his cloak streaming in the wind, made off at speed in the direction of Dover. The rest followed in as orderly a fashion as they could. The crowd, seeing its victory, shouted after them, and the sticks and the stones flew through the air to drop in an ugly shower behind the flying hoofs of the last horse.

Delirious with triumph, the crowd now began to conduct the Archbishop and his following up the beach. Someone had found horses for the bulk of the party, but these made little difference to the speed of the journey, for it turned now into a triumphal procession.

Ever since John of Salisbury landed in England, word of the Archbishop's return had been spreading throughout the countryside. For days, now, the people had been awaiting him, peering out across the sea for a sign of his boat, eying the unfavorable weather morning by morning, shaking their heads— waiting and waiting for the moment when they would greet him. As soon as the ship was sighted and identified beyond a doubt by the archiepiscopal cross held proudly in the bow, messengers had set out for every parish in the diocese. So by the time the Archbishop started along the six-mile journey from Sandwich to Canterbury, every parish priest at the head of his own people waited to welcome and do honor to the returning prelate. Mostly these were the poor of the county, laborers and the like, for whom Thomas Becket's name stood as a symbol of courage in adversity, of defiant strength in the face of tyranny. But there were, too, many more solid folk—farmers and their wives, squires of manors, burgesses and their families.

Beside the Archbishop's horse, small boys ran shouting, their sisters danced for joy at the roadside. Many devout persons dragged off their cloaks and capes and spread them on the ground before him. Others, more agile and less well endowed, pulled great branches from the trees and laid them down. And though it was winter, yet there still hung some shriveled, reddish leaves upon the beech and oak, to mingle with dark yew, with sharp-spined holly and great ivy swags. Every church bell was clamoring a welcome, and sometimes at the roadside crosses, the people stood together and sang.

"Blessed is he who cometh in the name of the Lord!" they chanted. "Blessed is he—blessed is he!"

Perhaps this was the most splendid moment of Thomas Becket's life—this joyous welcome home after exile. As he rode his horse at the head of his train of followers, his face shone with a brilliant, magnificent happiness, a glow that seemed like the glow of the sun, or of many candles lit in rejoicing.

But splendid as was this wayside acclamation, Canterbury had even more to offer.

As they came within sight of the city, of the sturdy walls, the pile of the great church, the palace, the monastery, a huge throng rushed from the gates to meet them. They sang and shouted and wept, they called for their Archbishop's blessing. They urged him forward among them, bringing him home to his church that had lacked him too long. Every citizen had decked himself in his best. At every window hung silks and carpets in joyous decoration. The bells of Christchurch clashed and clamored on the clear air of the winter's day.

Entering the city walls, the Archbishop pulled in his horse and dismounted. He stooped and put off his sandals. Barefoot, with his cross borne ahead of him by the faithful, fiery Llewellyn, Archbishop Thomas made his way along the last streets to his home.

He came within the precincts. There the monks of Christchurch awaited him. They surged forward— then hesitated; doubtful perhaps of his greeting, since in his absence many had had inevitable communication with men proscribed and excommunicated. Of these poor sins, it was true, John of Salisbury had seen fit to absolve them. Yet a natural delicacy restrained some at this moment from rushing forward to surround their father and call for his blessing.

Among the sea of faces, all above the familiar habit, were some old and remembered; older now, as his face was older. But others were young and wondering, too young to have known him except by repute, and awed, now, at his coming.

The Archbishop entered his church by way of the cemetery and went straight to the patriarchal throne. His face still wore that glow of immense contentment. Within the church, men were weeping for joy. The candles were lit. The choir raised a great ecstatic voice. The Archbishop held out his arms to his brethren, and as they filed past him he bestowed on each monk, of whatever rank or standing in the community, that kiss of peace denied him by the King who had once been his dearest friend.

Herbert of Bosham moved close by his master. He spoke to him softly, so that only those about them heard what he said:

"My lord, it is now no matter when you depart. Christ conquers—Christ reigns—Christ rules."

The Archbishop turned his glowing face to his old friend. He seemed about to speak, then smiled and said nothing.

They began to move from the church to the chapter house.

"Now he will preach," Eustace said to Simon, who had regained his side after the confusions of the journey from the coast.

Simon looked at the young man he had known so recently as a mischievous, cynical scholar. There was in Eustace's face a reflection of that glow that filled the Archbishop's. A faint, sad sensation of envy touched Simon. He remembered the first time he had seen the Archbishop—how he had fallen on his knees, saying *Father!* and feeling that all his troubles were at an end. How there had been all the marks of remembrance to keep his spirits high. . . . He would not admit that Eustace, in the full flood of his newly acknowledged vocation, was nearer at that moment to Archbishop Thomas than he, a poor young clerk in exile, had ever been. . . .

"Hush!" said Eustace, as though Simon had been speaking his thoughts. "Listen, now. . . ."

The Archbishop stood before them and a great silence settled over all those crowded within the walls of the chapter house. Then Thomas Becket gave them his text.

"We have here no abiding city; but we seek one to come. . . ."

As he followed Master Herbert down the nave next morning after mass, Simon thought he had never seen any church more magnificent. Not Pontigny, nor Vezelay, nor Sens, nor even Bourges, the grandest churches he had seen in France, could compare that morning with Christchurch of Canterbury. The morning was cold and fine, a thin sunlight slanted through the high windows. After the excitements of the day before, an immense peace lay over the church and the monastery, and over the palace of the Archbishop.

"Though not for long, I fear," Herbert of Bosham said to William Fitzstephen, who was walking besides him. "The disturbances will soon begin."

"We must trust in Heaven," Fitzstephen replied, in the slightly rebuking manner he so often used toward Master Herbert.

"Have I suggested otherwise? But these things are already known. *He* knows them. We also must accept what is to come."

Before the palace, they found a bustle of men and horses.

"Officials of the King," they were told. "And the chaplains of the sentenced bishops. They demand to see the Archbishop."

"Well, he is here to be seen at last," replied Herbert of Bosham, mildly. "Conduct them in without delay. No, wait—I'll be their guide."

He strode up to the crowd and at once the leader pushed forward to meet him. But there was something far more formidable in the tall straight stillness of Master Herbert, than in the aggressive stance of the King's man who thrust up to him.

"Where is the Archbishop? We are to speak to him in the King's name."

"But the King is in France."

"We are his men in England, and we have to answer to the Young King for the peace of the realm. The Archbishop comes here not in peace, but with fire and sword. He treads his fellow bishops underfoot. He treats them as his footstool."

A faint smile flickered over Master Herbert's handsome face.

"I will take you to the Lord Archbishop," he said. "It would not be fitting that he should hear this from anyone but yourself."

The officials and the chaplains went indoors, attended by various of their clerks and servants, their boots making a great clatter as they crossed the threshold and went into the hall of the palace. William Fitzstephen followed after them, and Simon was left to go and get some breakfast.

He was late. The refectory was cleared and empty, so he went to the kitchen. There was one old monk pulling loaves from the oven and the whole place smelled of hot bread. Simon's mouth watered. Although he was accustomed to a long fast, he felt suddenly faint, so that he leaned heavily against the great scrubbed table in the center of the floor.

The old monk looked up, and at once left the steaming loaves and went to those cooling on a tray at one side. He broke one in four and handed a piece to Simon.

"Who's this wearing a cowl and fainting for hunger?" he demanded. "You've a long way to go, brother, if you're to be one of us here in the priory of Christchurch."

"I am clerk to Master Herbert of Bosham," Simon explained as he munched. "I am not a novice, even—"

"But you're every inch of a hungry lad!" the old man said, chuckling suddenly. "Eat up, brother. There's milk in the pitcher by the door. Take a beaker from the shelf. Though it is Advent, and there'll be a thin dinner for us all, there's no call from Heaven to make yourself ill. Here"—he kicked a stool forward—"sit down."

"God bless you, brother," said Simon, grinning back at him gratefully. "It was a long journey yesterday. I cannot find my way about this place—I walked two miles, I swear it, before I reached the church."

"You will soon get used to it. Sit down, I tell you. You may pay for your bread and milk by the tale of your exile."

"Why," Simon cried, sitting down on the stool as he was bidden, "I should not know where to begin."

"Anywhere you please, brother. Come now—speak up."

Between munching his bread and drinking his milk, Simon began to tell something of the times in France. Long before he was halfway through, and had finished the better part of the loaf, two lay brothers had come in from the dairy and stood listening. Then the cellarer came and joined them. They stood round attentive and silent, only sometimes exclaiming in amazement or approval at what he told.

Suddenly Simon was filled with the immense pleasure of self-importance. He had never had so many people listening to him before. Great quantities of words seemed to fill his brain, and from them he chose what he pleased. It was like being presented with the key to a treasure-house. He had had no idea how much there was to tell, how he could so present the tale that he had them all hanging on his next word. He had seen so much and heard so much—and he knew much more that he was not at liberty to include in his tale. He spoke of the terrible winter journey to the coast. He told them about Pontigny and of his first sight of Archbishop Thomas. He could even tell them about the King's court.

"There my brother is employed. He is like me in face though not so like as might be. He is ruddy, where I am pale. And he is stronger altogether than I. He rides any horse in the world, and he carries a hawk as proudly as the King himself. We are twin, and should never have been parted."

"God's will be done, brother," said the old monk gently. "Tell us how the King and the Archbishop met at last, and how the King of France himself was their mediator."

Simon thought for a moment. Then the words came. They flowed from him as easily as if they had first been written down and committed to memory. His audience shifted nearer. It was swelled by the porter, who was passing through the kitchen and paused when he heard what was going on. Gradually they all settled down, as though there was no other purpose for them than to listen to every word Simon spoke. Their eyes never left his face. With quick intakes of breath and exclamations, they gave him every proof a storyteller could have asked for that his skill was considerable.

Suddenly he broke off and hurried away, in a panic lest Master Herbert should by now be calling for him. His mind was light with an unfamiliar excitement. He felt that he had dug up a buried talent that he might one day spend to advantage. How? His heart thumped as he hurried to find Herbert of Bosham. He half knew that the talent should go to pay a debt. . . .

He came suddenly on Master Herbert talking with Prior Richard of Dover and several others Simon could not name. They stood a little beyond the door of the Archbishop's room and spoke in low voices. It needed only a glance to reveal that the joy of yesterday's homecoming had already fled. In fact, the disturbances foretold by Master Herbert had already begun.

It was now only a few days until Christmas and the usual preparations for the feast occupied the monks of

Christchurch. Apart from spiritual preparation, they had some physical duties to carry out. Every monk was obliged at this season to take a bath. The shaving of tonsures, which ordinarily took place once in three weeks, was to be held back a few days that all might be neat for the feast; the psalms that were always recited in the process of this rather tedious business would be specially chosen for the season.

Not only the offices of Advent and the coming of Christmas occupied the Archbishop. He had sent away the bishops' chaplains firmly enough—but he had promised that he would now intercede on their behalf with the Pope, so long as they took a vow to accept in all humility the final judgment of His Holiness. With this news, grumbling, the chaplains had set off to seek their masters in France, where they had hastened to gain the ear of the King.

The Archbishop was anxious to see the Young King without delay, that there might be no occasion to doubt his loyalty. The Court was then at Winchester. It was therefore decided that Prior Richard of Dover should ride there to tell the Young King that Archbishop Thomas was coming himself to pay homage to his new sovereign. Thomas Becket remembered his one-time pupil with affection, and he sent him by Prior Richard a present fitting to his youth and spirit. Three magnificent chargers he selected himself, and with them all the splendid trappings usual to a war horse. Yet when Prior Richard returned to Canterbury it was with news of a discourteous reception.

"I was instructed to say to the Archbishop that he

need not go to Winchester. The Young King will send his own messengers to the Archbishop in his own time."

Aware that he might intercept these messengers in London, the Archbishop rode to the capital with a stern face. All along the route he was greeted as he had been greeted on his way to Canterbury from the coast. An immense multitude came three miles out of the city to meet him and conduct him within the walls. The Bishop of Rochester, an old friend, brought all his chapter and clergy. At the city gates there was another procession, this time made up of the canons-regular of St. Mary's, Southwark. Bells rang, singing filled the air. *Te Deum* sounded on all sides, and all the scholars and students were in the streets.

Yet as the procession from St. Mary's gathered up the Archbishop and led him toward their church, a single voice cried sudden and clear out of the crowd.

"Archbishop—Archbishop! Beware of the knife! Beware—beware of the knife!"

The Archbishop sent to know who it was calling out in warning.

"It is a woman named Matilda," he was told. "She is out of her mind, and has been this year or more."

The dismal cry seemed to echo long after the woman had been left behind, and the church of St. Mary had received the Archbishop and his following.

The Young King's promised messengers came to London the next day and sought out the Archbishop there. One of these was Josselin of Arundel, the King's uncle; with him came Thomas Turnebuhe, a knight. It was a poor sort of embassy, an insult in itself.

"The Young King bids you return to Canterbury, Archbishop," said Josselin of Arundel. "I bear the royal command, which must be obeyed."

The Archbishop sat in his great chair and his stillness made him seem a man of stone, for all the splendor of his gown and his great jeweled ring.

"Is it the Young King's intention to shut me out from his presence?"

"His commands are as I have told you," replied Josselin of Arundel. "That is all my message. Farewell, Lord Thomas." He went from the chamber without further salutation, turning his back as though on a servant. The door was still open when he was heard greeting a man in the antechamber, a rich London merchant who had come to pay his respects to the Archbishop. "What?" he cried. "Are you come to the King's enemy? I advise you to return home with all speed."

Then someone shut the door and the reply was lost.

From this moment there seemed to be a closing of the ranks against the Archbishop. The Earl of Cornwall, another of the Young King's uncles, had always been a friend. From him there came a most urgent message. "Nothing is safe," said he. "Tell this to the Archbishop. And to all those who are with him—wherever they are they are like to be killed."

Thereafter, when the Archbishop traveled, he took with him an escort of five mounted soldiers. But this was soon reported as being practically an army, in whose midst this enemy of the King moved about the countryside, terrorizing the inhabitants. Louder and fiercer grew the complaints of those about the Young King, and those who stood as his father's proxies in England. Then there came petty persecutions from Ranulph de Broc and his brother Robert. They hunted in the Archbishop's forest, which was forbidden by law. They seized a ship of his, coming with a cargo of wine from France. They waylaid a train of his servants, and mutilated one of the horses by cutting off its tail. . . .

All this was the more intense in effect because it was crowded into a little space, into the few remaining days before Christmas.

On the eve of the feast, the Archbishop said mass at midnight, and on Christmas Day he celebrated high mass at the great altar of Christchurch, flanked by the twin altars of St. Dunstan and St. Alphege, whose relics sanctified their shrines. It was splendid to watch him moving about the altar, magnificently vested, in the great high church. He seemed far from Simon now as, a mere member of the vast congregation, he recalled the dim early morning at Pontigny in the chapel of St. Stephen. The voice that had murmured then in amazement and joy, rang out now above their heads as the Archbishop mounted to the pulpit and gave his Christmas text: *On earth peace to men of good will.*

He seemed at that moment the epitome of all churchmen, triumphant, confident, benign. . . . Yet barely an hour later they were saying that he had wept openly in the chapter house, speaking of his own death and saying that Canterbury would soon add another name to her roll of martyrs. . . .

Later still, he cast off his mood of doubt and foreboding, he became almost jovial. The rest of that Christmas Day passed as such a high and holy festival should. It was a Friday, but the day's abstinence was set aside in honor of the feast, and they dined well, Archbishop Thomas in their midst. A tranquillity that most knew to be false settled over the whole community.

Two days later, on the feast of St. John the Apostle, Simon was already in bed when he was summoned to Master Herbert in the palace. He roused himself with difficulty. A cold moon stared out of a sky deep with frost. He pulled on his clothes, then fumbled his way along the dark passages and came at last to the room where Herbert of Bosham would be waiting.

He was entirely unprepared for what he found. Herbert was on his knees by the hearth. He was praying in a muttering undertone. His eyes were closed, but in spite of this tears were running down his face. He was wringing his hands together and rocking himself backward and forward, as though his misery could not be contained.

For a second Simon had the appalling thought that some murderer had already fallen upon Archbishop Thomas and slaughtered him. It was this that made him bold, so that he rushed forward and seized Master Herbert by the shoulders.

"Brother!" he cried. "Oh brother, tell me, tell me!"

Herbert of Bosham grasped Simon's hand. He pulled himself to his feet and said in a mumbling voice: "I am sent into France. I am to go to King Louis and tell him of the peril here."

"When must you go?" Simon asked, dismayed. He did not like the thought of losing this rock of a man at such a moment.

"At once—and by night, for fear of treachery. Yet it is all for nothing that I am to be separated from him—for I know I shall not see him in the flesh again. For this, God forgive me, I am bound to weep. I was determined to abide with him cheerfully to the end—for it must come soon. Now I am sent away."

"Alas, alas! Does his lordship know of your fears?"

"He knows, Simon—he knows. He says that what I mourn is true indeed—I shall *not* see him in the flesh again."

"God save us all," said Simon, shivering. "Am I to go with you to France?"

"No—it is better that I go unattended. Llewellyn also goes, with Gilbert Glanville. But they are bound for our Holy Father the Pope, and they bear letters. . . . I have summoned you from your bed because I need help in my preparations. And because I trust you to take my place in any alarm. Does that sound foolish? I have known you since you were a child and you are a child no longer. You must take all you are able to of a man's part in whatever may happen. You must witness what I cannot."

"I will do all I am able," Simon replied, steadily. "And do you fare well in your mission, Master Herbert, and return to us safe and soon."

"Please God, and amen," replied Herbert. "Now— go to the kitchen and find me some bread for my satchel. Take a light from the porch. Make haste. They are already seeing to the horses."

There was a great scurrying to and fro of those concerned with seeing off the travelers. A chill wind blew round the cloisters and whistled about the palace gateway. Soon the horses were being walked in the court before the side door of the palace. Then Llewellyn came out, grumbling, speaking sharply to the grooms, complaining that the time was passing and the night not dark enough. He was joined by Herbert of Bosham and Gilbert Glanville. They mounted at once, and in a matter of seconds the clatter of hoofs on the pavement had changed to the less defined clop and slither of iron on cobbles as they rode through the city streets.

Simon stood at the gate, which the porter was already closing, as though he could still see the horsemen on their way. But now even the sound of hoofs was carried away into distance and silence. He turned and went back into the palace, to see that all was in order in Master Herbert's lodging.

As he crossed the hall, he noticed a tall monk standing near the door. Simon recognized him as

Edward Grim, who had come from Cambridge before Christmas to the Archbishop's household. His manner of quiet reverence and admiration, his strong sturdy good looks and humor, had given him an immediate standing in Thomas Becket's circle of devoted friends and servants.

The sound of the great key turning in the lock, and of bolts sliding home with a clang of iron into iron, made Simon pause and listen. Then the porter, his keys clanking together, his sandals slapping on the pavement, crossed the courtyard and moved off toward the cloisters.

"Now we are a besieged garrison," said Edward Grim.

He spoke quietly and without any particular emphasis. His simple words sounded with force and shock in Simon's mind. Truly they were within and the world was without, and the world was hostile. He wished the great gates might remain fast closed forever.

IX

Four Knights Set Out

"HERE THEY COME," said Hugh de Morville.
"Now we shall hear a tale of woe!"

He laughed. He swept up the chessmen and the
board and pushed them aside. Another move and he

131

would have lost the game; the interruption was very welcome. His opponent grimaced. But as he was only a subordinate at the King's court, he was silent. He put the chessmen into their carved coffer and carried them back to the great chest where they were kept. The chessmen were very old; it was said that they had been brought back from the East by a follower of Count Baldwin, when he returned from a Crusade.

"We'll finish the game another time," Hugh de Morville called after him. "Well—we'll play another game, then. And this time I'll set a wager—my golden chain with the holy amulet to that horse of yours you're always boasting about."

Edmund Audemer had no time to reply, for the chamberlain suddenly beat on the floor with his staff, everyone in the hall rose hastily, and the King came in with his usual vigorous stride. He threw himself into the great carved chair on its dais that served as a throne here in the palace at Bur, in Normandy. He pulled his robes into order and settled his cloak about him, for it was very cold. Then he leaned back in his chair and glared at those who sought an audience.

"Now!" he said. "Well? Speak! Speak, my lords— that is what you are here to do."

The Bishops of London and Salisbury glanced at one another and each seemed to wait for the other. It was London's prerogative and at last he found words.

"My lord King," he said, "we have come to you again in person to give weight to what we have to say. But we dare hardly speak, since we are excommunicate and hesitate to lay upon your Majesty any such sin as that of holding converse with us."

The King sat snapping and cracking his fingers and made no answer to this. But it was clear that had he chosen he would have replied extremely shortly. They had asked to be heard—he had come to hear them—and now they would not speak. . . . He looked from London to Salisbury, who in turn began making excuses.

"Indeed, my dear lord, I dare not address your Majesty for fear of the injury to your Majesty's soul. . . ."

The Archbishop of York, the third of the complainants who had suffered under the sentence pronounced by Thomas Becket with the Pope's authority, had entered the hall at the King's side. Since the departure of Archbishop Thomas for England, and since the sentences that had sent the victims scurrying back to France, it had been York who had most enjoyed the King's ear, York who had taken every opportunity to flatter and encourage. Unlike the Bishops of London and Salisbury, he was not excommunicated, merely suspended from his holy office until the Pope should see fit to reinstate him. Since this suspension came about because of his part in the coronation of the Young King, in which he had been urged and coerced by the King himself, he was in a strong position. Now he stepped into the breach left by his colleagues.

"The news is bad, sire," he told King Henry. "As your Majesty well knows, when these sentences were pronounced we came at once to court to tell you of our injuries. And since, we have sent our chaplains and spokesmen to the Archbishop of Canterbury to demand that the sentences be withdrawn—"

"And they were treated contemptuously!" broke in the Bishop of London in a sharp, angry voice, forgetting his recent concern for the King's soul. "I would the brother who has most to tell were here now—but the weather was bad when he crossed the sea. He is lying at the coast and he is abominably sick from the journey."

"But he would indeed convince your Majesty," agreed Salisbury. "He has such tales to tell of Archbishop Thomas—"

"Ah, that ingrate!" cried York. "It is not enough for him that your Majesty accepted reconciliation and allowed him to return to Canterbury. He must needs set about false tales to the Pope. He must needs excommunicate and suspend . . . why, he would dethrone the Young King if he could—for no other reason than wounded pride—it should have been *he* who placed the crown on the prince's head!"

"Then he is a traitor!" someone cried out.

At once there was a startled silence. The one word had been spoken that could never be recalled, but must echo interminably.

Edmund, who had recently been appointed cupbearer to the King, had taken from a steward the goblet and the wine that the King invariably called for as he sat in audience. He moved up toward the great chair, as he was expected to do. The King's hand, with its snapping fingers, reached out for the goblet. Edmund went down on one knee and poured the wine. It was as the wine came near the rim, still with no check from the King, that the cry of *Traitor!* sounded in the hall. The King's hand shook so violently that Edmund with difficulty prevented the wine from spilling over the fur-trimmed sleeve. He did recover himself, certainly, but so narrowly, and with so much awareness that it needed now only one such little thing to bring about disaster, that he heard his heart pounding in his ears. Whatever was to unleash the King's gathering wrath, let it, he prayed, be no fault or gesture of his.

"Well, well," said Roger of York, as though in deprecation, "words are easily spoken. But it is sure the Archbishop's wrath is turned on all who set a crown upon the head of the Young King."

"By God's eyes," swore the King, "if all who were concerned with my son's coronation are to be excommunicated—then I must be one of the number!"

He gave a great bellow of angry laughter. This time no one spoke. They all knew how near he had been to the sentence more than once, and how by the chances of time he had avoided it.

"We have heard from Ranulph de Broc in Kent," said Hugh de Morville, "how the Archbishop luxuriates in the power his return seems to give him." He turned to one of the knights at his side: "Is it not so, FitzUrse?"

"It is true enough," replied Reginald FitzUrse. "We

have heard, sire, that this Archbishop is riding about the countryside with a great armed band—as though he were a prince or even a king."

"Trying to win for himself castles and fortresses," put in another who was standing there, whose name was Richard Brito. "This we have heard in silence until now, my good lord, for fear of rousing wrath against the Archbishop. We all know that he was your Majesty's friend in better days—the object of your Majesty's great generosity, as he is now of your clemency. Ah, my lord, you should not have been persuaded to let him return to England!"

The King muttered and thumped with his clenched hand on the arm of his chair. He drank down his wine and held out the goblet to be refilled. Standing as he was a little behind the chair to anticipate the King's wishes, Edmund could see how his neck was reddening, how it seemed to tighten and throb with the strength of his mounting anger.

"Have patience, sire," said the Archbishop of York. "Truly the storm cannot be turned aside. But we must have patience. It is best that he should go on in his own way for the present."

"But what, then, would you have me do?" demanded the King in a great voice, "Am I to suffer his insults in silence? Tell me—advise me! You are my bishops!"

"Sire, sire," cried the Bishop of London, "it is not for us to advise you! It is not our place or our duty."

"Let your barons and your soldiers advise you,"

said Salisbury. "We cannot tell what course should be taken."

"There is only one way to deal with such a fellow," cried one of the barons, de Bohun, who was Salisbury's uncle. "Plait enough withies to make a rope—and hang him!"

This time there was a shock of terror and excitement over the entire court. It ran into a second's silence, then broke in whisperings and murmurings, in nervous titters and uneasy attempts to quiet de Bohun, who seemed pleased with the sensation he had created.

"It is not the first time," agreed William of Malvoisin, another baron, "that a churchman has been killed for his insupportable insolence and pride."

"Certainly," agreed the Archbishop of York in a low voice, as though the admission was wrung from him with infinite and bitter sorrow, "so long as Thomas Becket lives you cannot hope for tranquil days."

Edmund was watching the King warily. Now the redness in his neck had mounted and touched the scalp where the hair was thinning on the crown. Now his right hand thumped almost rhythmically on the chair arm. Once more his left hand, holding the wine cup, was thrust out toward Edmund.

Usually he was a moderate drinker, but now all moderation was leaving him. There were increasingly significant glances among those about him. It was clear that one of his passions was coming upon him, and at such a moment none could tell what he might do or say.

Now the wine jug was suddenly empty, as empty as the goblet held out once again. Edmund looked apprehensively for the steward, but he had vanished. Everyone else was concerned with the King's condition, with the rash words of de Bohun and Malvoisin —and with the general tension and excitement, which was so great, so nearly hysterical, that it needed only the slightest thing to send it toppling over the edge of frenzy.

"Wine," muttered the King. "Wine!"

Edmund said hastily, "Sire, I am fetching more!"

"More? You are fetching more? Am I to wait while my cupbearer runs to the cellars? God's truth, I am poorly served!"

"My lord, the wine is less than usual," Edmund said. "Or this is the smaller jug. Yes—that is the reason it must be refilled. It is the small jug."

"And who brings it, save my cupbearer, Edmund Audemer? Do I keep you here at court for your mistakes, you whelp? No—and I'll do so no longer! There's your cup—take it!" He hurled the goblet in Edmund's face, and the few dregs of wine shot into his eyes. The goblet itself struck hard against his temple, then glanced off his shoulder and fell to the floor. "Now—tell whosoever pleases to hear that you were once in the King's service and are so no longer. Leave me! I took you for charity—for the sake of your father, who was a poor man for all his honor. For charity I took you in—for charity, then, give me some peace from your company! You are no longer any man of mine!"

He was shouting now and he had tottered to his feet. Yet it was not the wine that made him reel. It was common enough for the King to revile his servants, less so for him to insult his gentlemen attendants. The court waited, strained, humming with anticipation, to see what Edmund would do, what more the King would say—whether his fury would break in some harsh sentence on the young man, imprisonment, or some cruel punishment that would send him into the world maimed for his failure to pour wine for the King because at that moment there was no wine to pour. . . .

Before Edmund could speak, or move, or even think what was happening, the King gave a great roar of fury and shouted out at them all:

"I am poorly served! Poorly indeed! Not a cup of wine in my own hall and not an honest man among you. Curse on you all! Curse, I say! A curse light upon every one of you—false knaves that I have maintained under my roof at my own bitter cost! Here you see me plagued and tormented—and is there not one among you, you cowards who eat daily at my table, who will not serve me as I should be served? Is there none among you will save me from this low-born cleric who destroys my peace and my days in the land? What slothful wretches attend me here in my palace, that cannot of their loyalty take courage to come to my aid!" His voice which had changed from a roar to a bellow and now became nearer a scream, rang and vibrated in the hall, so that many cowered in fear. Only the cynical stood watching unmoved, waiting for the moment of collapse, when his body servants would carry him away to his bed. "God's curse on every one of you!" he ranted. "Rid me of him, I say! Rid me—rid me—rid me. . . ."

His voice died. He stood rigid a moment. Then he fell.

Instantly, the tension was released. As though a painted picture had taken on life, those in the hall relaxed, moved, turned to one another, spoke, smiled, frowned or even laughed. Three of the King's servants at once ran up and bent over him, wiping his brow and his slack lips, chafing his hands.

Edmund remained where he was. He could feel his face wet with the cold dregs of the wine and the warm trickle of blood from the cut on his temple. He felt dazed, inasmuch as he could not see clearly, yet wide awake in every hair and muscle as he realized that he was free—he was at liberty to take the King's word for his release and go away from his service forever. . . . He would do that—he would go. He would find his fortune elsewhere. He would go to England and find his brother Simon, who was a clerk in the household of Archbishop Thomas Becket. . . .

As the name of the Archbishop came into Edmund's mind, he woke up completely. He looked about him as though choosing his way of escape. He must go at once, before any other left the hall on a mission he dared not give a name.

Standing as he was on the dais, he had a clear view of the floor of the great hall. He saw Reginald

FitzUrse with his hand on Hugh de Morville's arm. He saw him speak low in Hugh's ear. Then Hugh turned his head and beckoned Richard Brito. They moved close together, and then a fourth knight, William de Tracy, shouldered his way among the throng and joined them. They stood close together. They spoke in whispers. They glanced back over their shoulders as though to see if any had observed them. Then, quietly, they left the hall.

At once, Edmund sprang down from the dais and followed. He must keep the four in sight. He pushed his way through the crowd with difficulty. He reached the courtyard as they were crossing toward the stables and he ran after, keeping in shadow. His own horse, Violante, was stabled near Hugh de Morville's, and they had spoken together often about the beast.

Hugh turned as Edmund sidled toward Violante's stall.

"Who's there? Ah—it's you, Edmund Audemer. Lucky to be alive and free!"

"Yes, my lord," agreed Edmund, fretting to be away.

"Lend me your horse, Edmund. I've a long brisk ride ahead."

"He'll not answer to any hand or heel but mine," replied Edmund, quickly.

In the background he was aware that the other three knights were leading out their horses, and the thought crossed his mind that they must have had them saddled in readiness. . . .

"Yet you say he's swift," de Morville insisted.

Edmund realized that only boldness would do. He

drew near Hugh de Morville and said in an urgent voice: "My lord, it is true none but I can ride Violante. But with him I can reach the coast ahead of you and have a boat in readiness."

De Morville grabbed his arm. "You know so much?"

"I know what I see," replied Edmund. "Will you deny me this chance of regaining favor with the King?"

"Ride, then," said Hugh de Morville. "We shall not be far behind."

Edmund ran into Violante's stall and spoke softly to the horse. It was a fine beast for a mere attendant at court, but it had been a gift to him from one who had loved his father. Edmund worked swiftly to saddle up. In spite of the fact that this delayed him, he rode out of the stable yard within seconds of the departure of the knights. It was a fine clear night, cold and heavy with stars. Violante took to the darkness as a bird to the sky. On the brow of the first low hill, Edmund passed the four knights at a gallop so near to flight that he had left them far behind by the time Hugh de Morville had recognized him and reassured the rest.

The road from Bur to the coast was well known to both horse and rider, but there was a shorter route that crossed a river by way of a ford instead of a town bridge. That was the way Edmund chose in his desire to reach England ahead of the four knights bent, as he now well knew, on murder.

The keen wind of the gallop made his eyes run with tears and he felt the cut on his temple smarting in the cold. But his heart was filled with the splendor of his own freedom, as his mind was quick with urgency, with the need for haste and good fortune to carry him to England.

When he came to the ford, the first light was moving up the sky. At once he saw his mistake. Last time he had ridden this way in summer, when the river was low. Now in the spate of winter it hurled itself over boulders, gushed and boiled and made an easy passage utterly impossible.

Yet it was a small river, running upstream between high banks that made a miniature gorge. In the half-light, Edmund began urging his horse along the riverbank, climbing steeply after less than a hundred yards, seeking a place that Violante might take in his stride. To be so checked at this point made Edmund crazy with impatience and frustration. How could he have been such a fool as to attempt the shorter course? Now he had lost everything he had gained and the four knights would reach the coast ahead of him.

Perhaps his impatience made him careless, too eager to cross and be away. He found the place he thought would do and set Violante to the jump. The horse refused. Edmund tried again, and again Violante would not budge. Edmund gritted his teeth. He had to cross the river and get to Canterbury somehow. He wheeled the trembling horse, put him again to the jump and this time dug spurs sharply into his sides.

Violante rose then in a great stride, his strong neck outstretched and striving to obey, his fine mane flying.

In the same instant, Edmund knew what he had done. He should have been content with the animal instinct of the splendid creature he rode. Below him the gorge seemed suddenly to widen, to gape for victims. Edmund kicked free of the stirrups and bunched himself for what must come. Violante's forehoofs struck against the further bank and plowed through the crumbling edge. Edmund went over the horse's head. He heard a long high scream that was Violante's death cry. He gazed over the edge of the gorge and saw Violante lying ten feet or so below, his back broken over a huge boulder, the swift water combing out his mane and tail and dragging at his great body to carry it away.

X

The Last Day

A LITTLE BEFORE midnight, Brother Paul, the sub-
sacristan, passed through into the monks' dormitory to call the brothers to matins, the first office
of the day. He carried a taper, with which he would

145

light the four great cressets that burned one at each corner of the long chamber. Simon and one or two others had been given sleeping room in an antechamber until they could be better accommodated, for the arrival of the Archbishop with his large household had strained the capacity of the palace and so some of his people had to find places elsewhere.

Simon stirred and groaned as Brother Paul passed. It was one of those unworthy moments when he felt relieved he would never be a professed monk. And that made him groan again, because he felt ashamed. But bed was warm and comforting at that coldest hour of the morning. What day was it? He struggled with sleep and at last remembered that it was Tuesday, the twenty-ninth of December, at the end of the first year of a new decade, 1170.

He drowsed off again. Then someone plucked at his shoulder. He dragged himself up from his comfortable sloth and opened his eyes. He saw the round, rather fussy face of Brother Paul close above him.

"The Archbishop has asked for you. Hurry."

"Why?" Simon mumbled. "It is too early for mass. . . ."

"He is to say his matins in his own room. Hurry."

Still confused, Simon stared helplessly at Brother Paul. Then a sudden feeling of immense urgency seized him. He was instantly wide awake. He hurled himself from his bed and pulled on his clothes at speed, fumbling as usual, groping about for his felt slippers which seemed to have disappeared under the bed. Soon he was hurrying along the dimly lit corridors and stairways, across the courtyard and so to the palace. He reached the Archbishop's room with two or so minutes to spare until midnight.

The room was full. The usual close friends and counselors were there—John of Salisbury, William Fitzstephen and the rest. There was also the newcomer, Edward Grim, together with certain monks who had known Archbishop Thomas before his exile, and who had been employed about him in various tasks since his return.

Simon looked round for someone of his own standing, another of the young clerks, or a novice like Eustace, who had come from Pontigny and might therefore command special notice. But there was no one else there to whom he could move instinctively and find his place.

The Archbishop had glanced toward the door as Simon entered, as he might for any latecomer, then turned aside to reply to Grim, who had just spoken to him. Then he looked again from his great height over the heads of the rest and beckoned.

At first Simon thought merely that the Archbishop was waving him to a place, perhaps even rebuking his lateness. But he was most certainly beckoning. Then it must be to someone who had come even later than Simon, and he turned to find out who.

"The Archbishop is calling you," a monk at Simon's elbow said.

He moved at once. He recognized the moment for what it was—another of those marks of sympathy between the two of them, so incongruously matched—

the highest and the lowest in that community that contained so many. As he crossed the room in answer to the summons, Simon felt as he had felt at their first encounter. Now, as then, he dropped on his knees. "Father," he said, as he had said then; and he waited to feel the hand of the Archbishop laid on his head.

But then the moment changed, and it was as it had been at their second encounter, when Simon had gone to confession and found the Archbishop himself seated in the chapter house—for Thomas Becket stooped slightly, and took Simon's left hand in his right. Then he closed his left hand over it and held it firmly, as he had done on that earlier occasion. And he seemed to be praying silently, for his face was stern and withdrawn, though his eyes were still on Simon and his lips did not move.

Suddenly Simon knew that this was the last time Archbishop Thomas would take his hand, or would send for him, or would pray for him. He knew that he had been summoned this morning along with the rest, because the Archbishop wished to make certain that a good-by was said. This was what marked the day for its own, not the fact that it was Tuesday, or the twenty-ninth of December, or cold or warm for the time of year—but the fact that it was Thomas Becket's day, and would always remain so—his last on earth, that must end none knew how, save that it would be in disaster.

Simon made some smothered exclamation. He

caught at the Archbishop's strong clasping hands and held them urgently, staring into the stern face and trying without words to express his understanding and his humble love.

Thomas Becket smiled. He released Simon's hand and gave him a quick blessing. Then he turned away, for the bell for matins was now ringing and the office must begin. . . .

That hour passed for Simon less in prayer than in anguish. In spite of himself, he was frightened. The foreknowledge of death in the Archbishop's face, and its calm acceptance, made his heart thump with terror. He kept thinking *How many of us, then? How many of us must die?* Perhaps all in this room had been chosen? And just as he knew himself unable to become a monk or a priest, how much less was he able to contemplate the idea of death, even though it might be a kind of martyrdom? He kept thinking of Edmund, longing to run away to find him—then sternly and bitterly rebuking himself. He was not a child any more. He had been brought to this point by a series of events far outside his control. He was old enough, therefore he should be strong enough, to accept his place or to reject it utterly. He was far too old to wait in terror for what was to come. The least he had to offer was his own steady loyalty— and that must content him.

When at last the Archbishop rose from his knees, he went to the window and looked out. The black night pressed coldly round the walls.

"What time is it?" he asked suddenly.

William Fitzstephen replied, "A little after one o'clock, my lord."

"How far is it to Sandwich? Could a rider be there by daybreak?"

"Why, it is only seven miles," said one of the others, uneasily, exchanging glances with his neighbors. "A rider could be there and back and there again long before daybreak."

"Then let any who wishes set out now."

There was a stunned silence. Though he had warned them often enough, this was the first inescapable word that told them what he recognized and accepted about this day.

"There is none wishes to ride that way," said Edward Grim, quietly. "Unless your lordship is one of the party."

But he shook his head. He muttered to himself, "God's will be done in me. I will await what must come in the church."

Then he turned from the window, as though everything was decided. Almost immediately, the bell was ringing again and it was time for lauds.

There hung over that day a strange, intense stillness, a sensation of waiting that silenced talk and quieted the footsteps of those moving about the palace and the priory and the church. The community existed in a state of suspension. None spoke of what might happen next, for it was not necessary. All knew, accepted and waited.

Yet nothing untoward marked the morning or the early afternoon. The Archbishop attended the morning's high mass. When it was over, he made one of his customary progresses of the altars and shrines of the saints, beginning with St. Dunstan and St. Alphege, and passing on through all the rest honored under that roof, until he came to the Lady Chapel. There he prayed in silence for some while, for the Mother of God had always commanded his dearest devotions. Afterward he went to the chapter house and was there with his wisest monks and advisers for longer than usual.

Among the younger members of the household there began to run a murmur of frightened speculation. The Archbishop was said to have made his confession, to have discoursed searchingly, to have been even more than usually devout, to have humbled himself to the utmost.

"It is a preparation," one novice said to another. "Has he not said already that this great church has one martyr and will shortly claim another as its own?"

"How?" someone said. "When?"

The answer was *Today*—but they were not strong enough to make it. Their youth and inexperience made them alert to the point of tension. They whispered in corners and scattered guiltily when a senior came by.

At three o'clock the Archbishop went to dinner in the great hall of the palace. With him sat various of his clerics and monks, divided on either side of him.

He ate well, and they noted this, commenting with satisfaction when he set about a pheasant.

"Thank God," said one, "I see his lordship dines more heartily and cheerfully today than usual."

The Archbishop, overhearing, laughed as he replied, not sparing their feelings or his own: "A man must needs be cheerful who is going to his Master."

He drank more wine, too, than was usual; this also was remarked.

"He who has much blood to shed," said Thomas Becket, "should drink much."

And again he laughed, though gently because of their troubled expressions. Of them all he was by far the calmest now. They were all lost in their terrible uncertainty. Their fear mounted as the afternoon light was absorbed in the increasing dusk and the place grew full of shadows. In many hearts there moved the dread of being found wanting, of lacking courage for whatever might be demanded of them. Yet as the time wore away and nothing happened, they began to rally a little, hopefully. Perhaps the perils had been exaggerated, perhaps the knocking on the door that everyone knew must come, would be the knocking of the King himself, hotfoot from France to bestow at last the kiss of peace upon his old friend....

When the Archbishop rose and went to his own room with a few of his friends, the lower servants and those who had waited on the high table sat down to their own dinner, Simon among them. There was a horde of beggars in the courtyard who would be given the substantial remains of the dinner, with bread in a very fair proportion, and the noise they made was their usual noise. They at least seemed to know no apprehension—though indeed the porter had spoken of rumors in the town that the Kentish castles were being manned; while one man outside the gate had declared that the King was sending soldiers to occupy Canterbury "because of Archbishop Thomas."

"Who's this?" Simon said suddenly, to one of the chaplains who was sitting beside him at table.

Four men were pushing their way through the crowd in the courtyard and into the hall. They wore surcoats with cloaks over them. Yet they had about them a harsh and iron look—the look of those men who had arrived on the shore at Sandwich and upbraided the Archbishop. There was no sight of mail, but there was this impression of hardness, and of the heavy movement of men in hauberks.

"They are armed!" Simon said in a whisper. He half rose in his seat, but the chaplain caught his arm and pulled him down.

"Wait!" he said.

Now the strangers were invited to dine, as was the custom in the halls of great men—but they thrust aside those who courteously addressed them.

"Where is the Archbishop?" demanded the tallest among them, whose surcoat carried a device of bears.

"That is Reginald FitzUrse," someone said. "He holds his lands from Canterbury. He is no enemy but a sworn vassal."

Thus they tried to reassure themselves. The four knights, however, continued to resist the welcome they were given. They thrust aside all who moved in their path. They pushed themselves in this manner to the doorway and up the stairs to the Archbishop's chamber.

"Move now!" the chaplain ordered Simon. "Move in behind them! Waste no more time!"

He rose and Simon with him, overturning the bench on which they had been sitting, so that it crashed to the ground. Simon ran to the stairs and leaped from steep step to steep step so fast that he reached the top long before the chaplain. The door of the Archbishop's room was open. He was sitting on his bed, discoursing with John of Salisbury. His other friends were all about him. As Simon came to the doorway, the Archbishop's seneschal, William Fitznigel, was announcing the strangers.

"There are four knights who come from the King in France, my lord. Will you speak to them?"

Thomas Becket looked up, turning from the monk at his side. The four newcomers were already pushing into the room, and his "Let them come in" was in fact lost in the bustle of their arrival.

The Archbishop remained seated on his bed. He looked from one to the other of the knights. He said, in a surprised manner, as though this was more than he had expected: "Is it you, William de Tracy?"

"Ay," he replied. And he added in a cold, contemptuous voice that was like the ringing of an alarm to every man there: "God help you!"

Reginald FitzUrse shouldered de Tracy aside.

"We are come to you with the commands of the

King. How will you receive them—in private, or in the hearing of all?"

"As you wish."

"Let it be as you wish, my lord," replied FitzUrse, shortly. "We are here to command you in the King's name—absolve the bishops!"

"There is nothing secret in this," said Thomas Becket, motioning back those who, torn between an instinct to give him privacy and a fear of leaving him with hostile men, had moved uncertainly to the door. "I did not suspend or excommunicate the bishops. It was done by the Pope. You should go to him."

"As you must go to the Young King and make your oath of fealty and swear to make amends for your treason!"

"What is my treason? I was on my way to the Young King when he ordered me home."

FitzUrse, increasingly the spokesman of the four, grew red in the face and began to shout his accusations.

"The bishops officiated at the Young King's coronation at King Henry's own command. Yet you call this treachery. Yours is an awful crime."

"Reginald, Reginald," said the Archbishop, gently enough, "I do not accuse the King of treachery!"

"This cannot be borne any longer!" shouted Fitz-Urse. "We are the King's liegemen, and we will not bear it any more."

The others broke in on that.

"We have stood enough, by God's wounds!" swore one.

"Stubborn and insolent! Traitor to the King's majesty!"

"From whom do you hold your title—answer us that?"

The Archbishop answered calmly, "Its spiritual rights and blessings from God and the Holy Father. Its temporal possessions from the King."

"Acknowledge that you have it all from the King."

"Not so—not so. I give to the King all that I owe him. But what is God's I will always give to God. If anyone injures the rights of the Church and refuses to make satisfaction I shall not wait for leave to do justice."

"These threats are too much," cried FitzUrse.

"Will he put the whole land under an interdict? Will he excommunicate us all?" demanded de Tracy. He pushed his face near the Archbishop's and cried, "We warn you. You have spoken to the peril of your life."

"Ah yes," agreed Archbishop Thomas, nodding his head, "I know you have come to kill me." He rose, then. He pulled himself up to his immense height and his great powerful voice rang out over their heads. "I make God my shield. If all the swords in England were pointed against my head, your threats could not move me. Foot to foot you will find me in the battle of my Lord."

The shouting of the knights, and the Archbishop's raised voice had increased the number of those within the room and in the antechamber and on the stairs. FitzUrse swung round on them and cried out:

"We order you in the King's name, whose liege-men we are, to leave this man!"

No one moved. The solid silent wall of monks and clerics, of servants and guests to the hall stood between the knights and the door. The four began pushing out of the chamber, calling as they went:

"We command you to keep him in safe custody until the King shall please."

Thomas Becket laughed suddenly. "I am easy to keep," he cried. "Do you think I want to sneak away? I did not come here to run away but to face the fury of cutthroats and the malice of impious men."

As he was speaking, he followed them to the door. He called to Hugh de Morville to come back and speak with him again, but de Morville would not turn. Though he had been far less aggressive than the rest, he followed them down the stairs.

In the Archbishop's room, which now cleared a little as some followed the knights to see what they would do next, John of Salisbury burst out furiously as though the silence he had imposed on himself was no longer to be borne.

"It is a wonderful thing, my lord," he cried, "that you will take no man's counsel. That a man of your station should so run after them and call to them. . . . They only try to make you angry. They seek nothing but your death."

"I know well enough what I ought to do, Master John."

"By God's blessing, I hope so."

"We have all to die, now or then. The fear of death must not turn us from justice."

"We are sinners and not ready for death," replied his old friend, sharply. "And I see no one here who wishes to die but you."

"God's will be done," said the Archbishop.

Everyone began talking suddenly. Some said the knights were drunk, that there was nothing to fear, nothing serious. But more were deeply alarmed. Two servants, crying that they would bar the outer door after the knights, rushed away down the stairs.

"Listen!" someone cried. "Listen!"

There was an instant of sharp silence. Far away below in the street was the sound of shouting, the clear fierce cry *"To arms! To arms! King's men!"*

Then at last they knew beyond doubting that there was to be no escape. On all sides there seemed to be the sound of hurrying feet, of men crying out in anger or in fear. The servants were running through the palace, they were bound for the safety and sanctuary of the church. Further off, there came a great crashing, as though someone was hammering at an obstruction, battering it down.

"It is the orchard door that the workmen have been mending," said one of the monks. "They will get in that way."

A young ostler rushed into the room. "My lord, my lord—they are arming!"

"What matter," said he. "Let them arm."

Robert of Merton laid his hand on the Archbishop's

sleeve. "You must go to the church," he said firmly. "There is no time to lose."

"No, no," he replied impatiently. "Do not fear. Monks are too timid."

"It is only right that you go to the church," insisted Robert. "The monks are at vespers. Will you miss the holy office, father?"

The Archbishop paused. He looked at Robert of Merton and very slightly smiled.

"So be it," he said. He moved forward, and they followed on a surge of relief. "No, wait—bear my cross before me as is right and honorable."

Llewellyn being far away, one of the others, Henry of Auxerre, seized the cross proudly and moved ahead of the Archbishop. A procession, orderly and commonplace, somehow formed itself out of the crowd of frightened and anxious men.

"Not that way, my lord!" cried Osbert, the steward. "There are armed men in the courtyard. We must use the other door." He looked around him swiftly and his eye fell on Simon, who was pushing along with the rest. "You are the youngest," he said, "and must be the fleetest. Run! Run round by the cellarers' lodgings and unbar the door there for the Archbishop. It is the better way into the cloister."

Simon at once began pushing and shoving himself out of the throng. He was obliged to thrust by the Archbishop and his crossbearer, and someone cried after him, even at that moment scandalized by his behavior. But he did not pause. Somehow he flung himself at speed down the treacherous stairway. Then, with the threat and clamor from the courtyard seeming to advance every second upon his heels, he was running along the dim passageway to undo the door and let through the Archbishop's procession into the sanctuary of the church.

XI

The Kiss of Peace

AS HE BROKE FREE of the press and started down
the stairs, Simon had not paused to consider
that he was new to this place and might miss his

way. Nor did he think of that now, running fast along the gallery away from the courtyard, where the tumult was still checked by the great gate that the servants had barred. He knew only that he was to go to a door and open it. His mind was so clear and so sharpened by the urgency of the moment that he had no doubt of reaching there in time. As though he had been moving about the mass and maze of the buildings for half his lifetime, he went without hesitation where he had been told to go. He found himself passing the cellarers' lodging. He shouted as he went by, in the hope that one of them might hear and come to help him. But it seemed most unlikely that anyone was in his place by now, save only those monks who had gone to sing vespers and would remain steadfastly to the end of the office.

Ahead of Simon suddenly was the door into the cloister, out of use for one reason or another, and bolted on the inner side—on his side, that is, away from the palace corridor along which the Archbishop and the rest would be by now proceeding.

The door was the usual stout oak door, studded with iron. It was gray and ancient and it looked strong enough to withstand the hammering of a thousand fists. It was closed with two great bolts and a bar of iron shot through iron sockets. There was no sign of a key. But peering at it he saw that the lock was not home. Either the key was lost or the lock faulty, and so the bolts and the bar had been called into use.

Simon, panting now, though he was hardly aware of it, flung himself at the door and began to wrestle with the bolts. There was a faint light from a lamp burning further along the cloister. The first bolt shot easily and he felt a great surge of triumph that made him want to shout. There was shouting enough, however, for the tumult of an increasing throng swelled louder with every second. The townspeople, he thought, must have come from their houses to discover what the confusion meant. They must be thronging at the palace gate in alarm.

The second bolt was higher and he had to reach up to it. He stretched up his right hand and dragged and eased. The iron was cold and his fingers slipped. None the less, he felt the bolt give very slightly and knew that only patience was needed. Patience, however, was the hardest thing he could hope for, with the seconds rushing away, with the Archbishop approaching, and with the four knights, most certainly armed by now and perhaps with more coming to their aid, forcing an entry somewhere out of sight. He eased himself up the door and heaved at the bolt once more. It began to move. It had rusted and it shrieked as he dragged at it, but it moved. Suddenly it shot back, pinching his fingers so that the skin was torn and the blood came quickly.

Now there was only the bar. Now, too, he thought he heard the Archbishop and the rest on the far side of the door. And he was right, for someone began shaking the door, as though to force it from that side.

"Wait!" cried Simon, heaving at the bar.

Behind him he heard footsteps. The cellarers had in fact emerged and were coming toward him. But they seemed uncertain what was going on, whether Simon was to be helped or hindered. He was aware of them holding back nervously. What did they think —that he was intending to let in the traitors?

It was imperative to waste no more time. The door must be opened. He called to the cellarers over his shoulder, but his voice was small and breathless now and lost itself in the noise from outside. He seized the bar with all his force, pushing and heaving, shaking it in a frenzy. It began to grind along through the sockets that held it. It needed only an inch more. He threw himself at it bodily—and the inch was won. He caught hold of the enormous door and dragged it open.

He was hurled aside by the surge of men who poured through the opening. Now there was no longer any pretense at order. The monks and the clergy alike had surrounded the Archbishop and were hustling him along, urging and imploring and praying.

"This way—this way! Ah, my lord—hurry—hurry! To the church—to the sanctuary!"

"Father!" they cried. "Father!" And they pulled at his clothes to drag him along, catching at his sleeves, at his arms, holding him about the waist. And all the time he protested and struggled to preserve his dignity, to make clear his courage to them and so put heart into them all. The whole swaying mass of them went pouring along the cloister to the chapter house, the Archbishop tall and stern in their midst, the cross still borne ahead of him, but swaying this way and that in the press. . . .

As the last of the monks passed and found the rest ahead, Simon struggled to his feet. He was stunned and exhausted and he could not clear his mind. He did not know what to do next, where to go, whom to look for. It was as though he had fulfilled a great mission in life and now was cast aside. At that his mind cleared a little—for was this the debt he had felt lay upon him, and was it now discharged? He looked vaguely at the immense door, thrust back on its great hinges. Hanging open, it showed its vastness as though for the first time. Yet he had opened it. He had laid hands on it and tugged it open. . . . He began to tremble and to shiver. For how had he opened it? He had laid *hands* on it? But he had only one. He remembered the cellarers, but he could not remember that they had helped him. Surely they had run up only as the door was opened, and been carried along with the rest into the church? He could not be certain—he could not remember, nor think. His teeth chattered. He thought he saw the truth but he was afraid to admit it to his mind because of all it must mean to him. Then he heard his own muttering and mumbling as he began to move after the rest, leaning against the wall to help himself along.

"Two hands," he muttered. "There were two hands. . . ."

But he held his limp left hand fast inside the folds of his sleeve and dared not draw it out because of his terror. He stumbled and nearly fell. He stood still a moment, trying to gather his strength. He must get into the church. He must go close by the Archbishop and then he would know. . . .

He began to run along the cloister. As he went, the tumult ahead and behind seemed to increase and beat in great waves about his head. Then he heard someone running behind him and he tried to go faster. He was desperately tired and longed to sink upon the ground and sleep. But the thought of the Archbishop drew him on, just as the running feet at his back drove him. He looked back once over his shoulder. Instantly, a voice called him by his name.

"Simon! Simon, wait! Wait for me!"

Simon knew at once that it was Edmund's voice that called, and his fear increased, for it seemed to him that he must be out of his mind. Edmund was far away, he was in France at the court of King Henry. . . .

"Wait!" the voice insisted.

Simon faltered to a stop. At once he felt an arm about his shoulder, clasping and supporting him. He knew then that by some miracle this was indeed Edmund who held him—so much taller and stronger than he, fearless and bold and strong.

"Edmund," he said. "Edmund . . . Oh brother, brother. . . ."

"I came to warn the Archbishop," Edmund was saying urgently. "Where is he? Have I come too late? There are four men set on to kill him. . . ."

"Yes, four—and they are here already. . . ." Simon grabbed at his brother and leaned against him, trying to recover himself. "We must go to him—we must go to him at once. Why did you not come sooner?"

"I would have been sooner. It is only by God's mercy I am here at all. . . . There is no time to speak of that now. Come—are you well enough? Come into the church."

There was a sound of men running behind them. Looking back, they saw a number of monks struggling in the opening of the door Simon had unbarred, struggling to hold back four men in mail and visored helmets who were thrusting a way through.

Edmund grabbed Simon by the wrist and urged him forward. They ran toward the door beyond the chapter house, the door through which the Archbishop had been hustled by his monks and clergy. But as they reached it, they realized that a number of men were still standing there, that they were beating on the door which someone had closed instantly the Archbishop entered.

"Too late," Simon said. "We must go back and use the door beneath the tower."

As he spoke, the door was flung open and the Archbishop himself stood there. He was protesting furiously to those about him. "On your duty of obedience, I bid you not to close the door! It is not seemly that a church should be made a castle." And he began pulling in those who had been left outside. "Come in!" he cried. "Come inside quickly! Quickly!"

The stragglers hustled in. Those monks clustered about the Archbishop began once more to drag him away, forcing him toward the steps up to the choir, and urging him to hide while there was yet time.

"Let me be!" he insisted. "Leave it to God. He knows his own business."

He turned and began to move without haste up the steps to the choir and so toward the high altar.

But as he reached the fourth step, the armed knights burst through the door and paused on the threshold, checked by the darkness and the whispering that seemed for an instant to fill the great building and then to die away.

Edmund held Simon so hard that he almost sobbed. He had dragged his brother to crouch in the dark under the steps beyond the Lady Chapel, and although Simon struggled to escape, Edmund would not let him go. He put his hand over Simon's mouth. Simon struggled and writhed, the tears ran down his cheeks, but Edmund would not let him go.

"Be silent, you fool," he whispered close in his ear. "Do you want to be killed in your turn?" He took away his hand. "I do not want to hurt you. But understand—there is nothing you can do—nothing."

"I could take his hand!" Simon cried, choking. "I could take his hand now. . . ."

Somewhere in the dark nave, where only a few small lamps burned to show the merest outlines of vault and pillar, there was a crowd that huddled in silence and terror. Those who had surrounded the Archbishop, who had pressed in with him and urged him to hide himself, had melted away one by one, their courage insufficient to protect him to the last. The singing of vespers, which had wavered on to its close in spite of everything, was concluded before the knights entered and had released its celebrants to scatter with the rest into the shadows. The choir was empty. The black hollow of the church was pierced by the little eyes of the sanctuary lamps burning before altars and shrines. There stood now with the Archbishop only three of all his following—Robert of Merton, his old friend and confessor; William Fitzstephen, the chaplain; and the newcomer, Edward Grim, who had seized the cross from the hands of Henry of Auxerre when he fled with the rest.

The knights stood entirely still in the doorway. A faint light touched their armor and their drawn swords. They hesitated to enter. A pillar, darker than the darkness, withheld the Archbishop from their view. Besides, this was a moment to make a man pause, if not falter altogether. Entering that place with drawn swords they had already committed sacrilege. How much further into sin must their next step take them? They waited, listening. Perhaps he would come toward them, and then they could drag him outside and kill him there; or merely take him their prisoner as the mildest among them, Hugh de Morville, had always counseled.

The silence held, it settled. It could not have been longer in fact than a few seconds, yet its weight was enough to crush a man nearly to death.

Losing his patience at last, Reginald FitzUrse took a step forward and shouted into the darkness, "Where is Thomas Becket, traitor to the King?"

His voice echoed among the vaulting and returned a score of times, but no one answered.

"Where is the Archbishop?" cried FitzUrse.

"I am here," he replied at once. "No traitor, but a priest of God. What do you want with me?"

As he spoke, he moved down the steps again and came toward them into the faint light of the altar lamps, appearing so suddenly that FitzUrse, startled, fell back a pace or two. The Archbishop passed him by, tall, calm, severe, and stood by the pillar that had until now hidden him.

"What do you want with me?" he said again.

At this FitzUrse recovered himself and cried: "Your death! It is impossible that you should live a minute longer."

"I accept death," replied the Archbishop, "in the name of the Lord. And I commend my soul and the cause of the Church to God and to his Blessed Mother, and to the patron saints of this church. I shall not feel your swords. But though you seek my life I forbid you in the name of Almighty God and under penalty of anathema to harm in any way any of these my people, monk or layman, high or low."

Hugh de Morville rushed forward and grabbed his sleeve. "Come—this way. You are our prisoner."

"I will not come!" thundered the Archbishop. "What you will do to me—do it here. Willingly do I embrace death—so be it the Church, through my blood, may come to liberty and peace."

In spite of being armed, the knights still hesitated.

Again they tried to seize him. William de Tracy, the strongest among them, attempted to drag him across his shoulders and carry him off thus. But the Archbishop thrust him off contemptuously, standing firm with his back against the pillar. When FitzUrse sprang at him, Thomas Becket, remembering his warrior days, seized him and hurled him to the ground.

When he saw this, Edward Grim set the cross aside and rushed forward, flinging his arms about the Archbishop to support and strengthen him. There was now no sight or sound of Robert of Merton, and none of William Fitzstephen. Only Edward Grim, who knew him less well than any and might therefore have been excused, stayed fast beside him. In the huge darkness the rest lay hidden, silent and ashamed and sick with sorrow.

Reginald FitzUrse took a step forward suddenly, holding his sword before him. Now he had made up his mind. There was no longer any doubt of how this must end, and his should be the vile glory of the first blow.

"Reginald, Reginald," said the Archbishop, "you owe your lands and property to me. Yet you come against me with a drawn sword—and in the house of God."

"I owe you nothing! My fealty is to the King. Die, then, traitor!"

His sword swept up. Edward Grim, wrapping his cloak round his arm, threw up his hand to parry the blow. The sword struck his arm so violently that he staggered and fell, crying out and groaning. But the blow continued in spite of being deflected, and struck the Archbishop on the side of the head.

"Strike! Strike!" shouted FitzUrse wildly to his fellows.

This brought Richard Brito forward, and he beat with the flat of his sword on the shoulders of the Archbishop.

From that moment, the fury of the murderers and their frenzy at the sight of the flowing blood, kept them striking blow after blow. FitzUrse and de Tracy and Brito stabbed and struck and hacked, while a few paces away Hugh de Morville held in check a crowd of townsfolk which had suddenly and silently surged forward up the nave, as though they would at least participate in the martyrdom. . . .

Simon had been quiet a long time. Now he made one last bid to break Edmund's grip. Taking him by surprise, he almost succeeded in leaping forward, but Edmund recovered and dragged him back. They began to scuffle together on the ground, silently and desperately, while above them in the chapel the knights, panting and grunting, strove wildly to subdue their victim.

For blow upon blow, Thomas Becket stood upright. Then at last he faltered and fell to his knees. He put his hands to his face and wiped away the blood from his eyes, and seemed to look with surprise at his wet palms. Then he folded his hands falteringly and slowly. His lips moved but his voice was silenced now. He fell forward, gently and with a strange unbroken dignity. Then he was still.

The knights staggered back and stared down at their handiwork. Richard Brito's sword was snapped and he tossed away the rest. A fifth man, who had come with them but remained all the time well in the background, now stepped forward. He was Hugh of Horsea, a renegade monk whose hatred of the Archbishop was deep and bitter. He drew his sword and struck at the skull of the dead man, scattering brains and blood on the pavement.

"Let us go!" he cried. "The traitor is dead! He will not rise again!"

Then they gathered their cloaks about them and hid their weapons, and rushed from the church shouting "King's men! King's men!" so that everyone fell away from them and none dared hinder or accuse them of the evil they had done.

Now in the church there was only the whispering of those who had hidden, and those who dared not approach nearer. And there was the faint moaning of Edward Grim as he dragged himself away, clutching at his wounded arm. There was no sound of weeping and no sound of any prayer to honor the man who had died. The body lay, bleeding still, close by the altar of St. Benedict. Its stillness was like the stillness of the church that held it, stone and marble, a stillness that would endure until time was ended.

Edmund felt Simon sagging in his grip. He released him gently. His brother lay against the steps with his eyes closed. For a moment Edmund wondered fearfully whether he had been too rough with the boy. But his brother stirred almost at once and opened his eyes, peering through the gloom into Edmund's face.

"Is it finished?" he asked in a whisper.

Edmund nodded.

"They have killed my father," Simon said.

For the first time since that day when his true father had died so violently, Simon clasped his two hands together and put his forehead down upon them, and wept bitterly.

"Come now," Edmund said after a while. "We must go to him. He is alone."

He helped Simon to his feet. There was still an intense silence in the church, but beyond there was a sound of shouting. Those of the townsfolk who had come into the church had now as silently left it. They had followed out after the knights, perhaps intending vengeance, though more probably only to shout curses after them.

"They are sacking the palace," Edmund said. "Simon, you must rouse up."

Simon shook his head as though to clear the tears from his eyes. Then he looked for a second at his two hands, but he said nothing. He went up the steps with Edmund and then fell on his knees by the body of the Archbishop.

Now at last there came a stirring within the church. Somewhere out of sight, Edward Grim was being tended. All at once, the place was full of the monks who had fled. They stayed beyond the chapel of St. Benedict, afraid, perhaps, to enter where sacrilege had been committed. They whispered and murmured and it was impossible to know whether they were praying for their dead leader, or consulting what next should be done.

"Someone is bringing a light," Edmund said.

"There is light enough to see what they have done," replied Simon, bitterly.

The light approached steadily and fast. Osbert came into the chapel. He stood looking down at the body. He was a sturdy, tough-minded man, and he did not weep.

"May their souls perish," he said in a low, fierce voice. Then he said to Edmund, "Hold the taper."

Edmund did as he was told.

"You must help me," Osbert said to Simon. "Take this knife and cut a strip from my shirt."

He pulled his shirt out and held the linen taut while Simon made a slit with the knife, and then between them they tore off a long band of linen.

Osbert knelt beside his dead master.

"Bring the light nearer."

Edmund moved close. Simon crouched down and put his hands as Osbert told him to on the poor shattered head, and Osbert bound it with the linen into some decency.

As he did so, Simon looked long on the face he would never see again. It was calm and untouched by pain or fear. The eyes were closed, the mouth seemed almost to move in a slight smile that was full of contentment and sweetness. There was a smear of blood down one side of the long arrogant nose and Simon wiped it away. He used his left hand, whose fingers still fumbled and shook, but which he knew was once more his own.

The monks began to move more swiftly about the church. The doors were barred. They came one by one to weep and pray over his body. They had abandoned him to his death, but had he not been determined on his own martyrdom as the only weapon left to him that he might use in the defense of his Church? The King who had so stubbornly refused him the kiss of peace would grant it now, groaning with remorse, to his memory. . . .

"Saint Thomas," someone said softly. And at once the word was taken up. "Saint—Saint—Saint Thomas of Canterbury—pray for us, thy brethren. Oh blessed Saint Thomas—intercede for us in thy glory. . . ."

Then they carried the body away to the crypt, where they must bury it too hastily for honor, but in the fear that the murderers might return and violate the martyr's corpse. Their sacrilege had desecrated the church. No mass would be said there for a year, the crucifixes and relics and the shrines would be veiled as for Lent. And though as always the Holy Office would be recited at the appointed hours, there could be no singing until the terrible offense was purged. . . .

Edmund took Simon by the arm and led him from the church, and they were silent together for a long time, walking slowly side by side in the dim chill cloisters. For Edmund the world would always be wide, and he was free now to come and go. But Simon

knew that the debt he owed to Archbishop Thomas
had become a thousandfold greater.

"He gave me back my hand," he said. "I think it is
perhaps the first miracle of the blessed St. Thomas. . . .
but tell no one, Edmund. Let it be forever between
him and me."

The End of the Story

IT WAS EDMUND who said they must leave Canterbury. He wanted to be on his way, and perhaps he felt that if he left his brother behind once more, he might not find him again. Simon, Edmund realized, needed looking after, and he had every intention of seeing to that himself.

"We could travel to Italy, Simon. We could find Goodman Godfrey and his family. Did you not say they are settled in Genoa?"

Simon nodded. "But I must pay my debt, Edmund. I have to write it all down, in my fairest hand, since it deserves only the best. I shall give this great story to the world—the story of Saint Thomas of Canterbury." He frowned, remembering. "I think I have known what I should do since the day Master Herbert called me *a witness*. And then, when I told the tale in the kitchen. . . ."

Edmund looked at his brother and smiled. What a simple creature he was, to be sure. Did he think none better than he would write of this great man? Would not Herbert of Bosham himself, and William Fitzstephen, and any one of half a dozen others who had known him well?

"You need only ink, pen and parchment," he said gently, "and the time to use them. All these we shall find at the end of our travels."

After a while, Simon admitted that this was so, and since all else he required was carried in his memory, he agreed that they should go. There was much that he longed to see of the world, and in spite of the years since he had seen Godfrey and Joan he thought of them almost as his own family.

Edmund had a little money, so they set out as soon as the weather allowed. On their way they heard much concerning the Archbishop, his death and his King. For the shock of the murder had sounded like a great thunderclap in the courts of Europe. Indeed, it had almost deafened King Henry, reaching him as a roar of vengeance. It was said that he wept and sobbed and swore that although the Archbishop's death must indeed be laid at his door, yet his intention had never been murderous. Unhappily, his friends and servants, seeing the alteration in his countenance and the flashing of his eye, had taken it upon themselves to interpret his fury and complaint as a command.

"Was it so?" Simon asked Edmund, when they heard this tale.

But Edmund shrugged and would not reply. He

felt a little strange, cut off from the life he had known for so long, and he remembered much of King Henry that he had admired; he preferred not to recall the rest. . . .

Meanwhile the tales grew at home in England of miracles and cures wrought in the name and by the relics of the murdered Archbishop. Gradually these accumulated into a mighty weight of clerical opinion that here indeed was not only a martyr but a saint. Soon the messengers were scurrying back and forth, between London and Canterbury, between Canterbury and Rome. Letters were written, pleas drawn up, councils convened, evidence sifted . . . and on the twenty-first day of February in the year 1173, a new saint, Saint Thomas of Canterbury, took his place in the calendar.

It took more than another year to bring King Henry to the shrine of the saint in the great church of Canterbury. Then to the tolling of bells, and in the awed and respectful silence of the city's inhabitants, he walked barefoot through the streets to do penance. Kneeling on the hard floor at the shrine, he submitted his bare back to the penitential scourges of the monks of Christchurch.

It was a moment of bitter defeat. He had sworn to repeal those laws against which Thomas Becket had stood out to the last. He would have sworn anything, perhaps, in those first moments when he realized what had been done in his name, and how he must stand in the eyes of the world. Now he had lost everything—his pride, his political advantage—and those

memories of a friendship he no longer dared to recall.

Staggering slightly, he appeared at the door of the
church, that the crowd should have witness of his
humility and pain. There must have been a very wry
thought in his mind at that moment. So far from de-
priving the Church, he had enriched her. He had lost
his own friend—but he had given the Church a saint.

Author Profile

BARBARA WILLARD (1909-1994) was born in Sus-
sex, England. She enjoyed over fifty years of writing
for both children and adults. Her father was an ac-
tor, and she made her first stage appearance at the
age of eleven. After completion of her formal school-
ing, she continued acting, and in addition, began writing film scripts and novels for adults. In the late 1950's
Miss Willard turned to writing for children, fulfilling
a life-long desire. Her favorite genre was historical
fiction. Since she had been an only child until the
age of twelve, many of her nearly sixty works reflect
a fascination with large families. Of her later work,
her personal favorites were the acclaimed *Mantlemass*
series, which follow an English country family from
the 1400's through 1600's.

If All the Swords in England was originally published by Doubleday in its Clarion Books series—a
special set of titles written to present significant historical times and events from a Christian perspec-
tive. Miss Willard also wrote *Augustine Came to Kent*
and *Son of Charlemagne* for this series.

LIVING HISTORY LIBRARY

The *Living History Library* is a collection of works for children published by Bethlehem Books, comprising quality reprints of historical fiction and non-fiction, including biography. These books are chosen for their craftsmanship and for the intelligent insight they provide into the present, in light of events and personalities of the past.

TITLES IN THIS SERIES

Archimedes and the Door of Science, by Jeanne Bendick

Augustine Came to Kent, by Barbara Willard

Beorn the Proud, by Madeleine Polland

Beowulf the Warrior, by Ian Serraillier

Enemy Brothers, by Constance Savery

Hidden Treasure of Glaston, by Eleanore M. Jewett

Hittite Warrior, by Joanne Williamson

If All the Swords in England, by Barbara Willard

Madeleine Takes Command, by Ethel C. Brill

The Reb and the Redcoats, by Constance Savery

Red Hugh, Prince of Donegal, by Robert T. Reilly

The Small War of Sergeant Donkey, by Maureen Daly

Son of Charlemagne, by Barbara Willard

The Winged Watchman, by Hilda van Stockum